To Dad and Jose Nieto (Father-In-Law) - two
of the wisest men I have ever known.

Both are deceased - This book is in their memory.

PREFACE

Wisdom can only be obtained in measurable quantities from experience and the process of aging. I suppose it is because at some point in life man quits following and worrying about his little head and commences using his big head.

There is an old German saying "Too soon we get old - too late we get wise (smart)" - you get the idea.

The characters in this book are purely fictional but each was constructed from a collection of wise men I have known over many years.

The setting is a rundown, abandoned filling station in Bugscuffle, Jack County, North Texas which this collection of characters converted into their domino parlor and club house.

I started this book around 1980 and did not complete it until 2012. It seems that every year I delayed publishing, some major event occurred that brought up subject matter for a new chapter. I finally had to just stop - before something else happened.

Bill Thomas

Judge Abraham ("Abe") Hardhart - Abe was a retired Federal Judge, having recently retired from the fifth circuit (New Orleans). He grew up around Kemp, Texas got a law degree at U.T. and practiced law for about 20 years before becoming a judge and when he retired he bought a little spread near Bugscuffle and built a house on it and started raising goats. He was seventy two years young and had been widowed about seven years. He was the Club's founder and of course, he was also the Club's resident expert on law and lawyers.

Billy ("Cowboy") Frankel - Billy was a cattle rancher - had been all his life. He was born on a ranch near Saint Jo about sixty years ago and graduated high school there - and that was the end of his "formal" education. They say he was the best football tackle ever to suit up in Montague county and turned down numerous scholarships and joined the Navy instead (cause he had never seen an ocean). When he got out of the Navy he rough necked in the oil patch a while and courted and married Lucy Bucy whose folks owned the largest ranch in the Bugscuffle vicinity. They died and Lucy was their only child; so Billy made the classic intelligent entry into the ranching business. Billy loved anything western and it was said that he had over 2,000 paperback westerns in his collection and had read them all - at least twice. Therefore, Billy was the resident expert in anything western (including sex and violence) and ranching. The group called him "Cowboy" and he liked that.

Antonio G. ("Tony") Gomez, M.D. (middle initial G. was for Gomez also) - Tony G. was born in old Mexico but his folks moved to Texas when he was young and he got his education in the U.S. (Tulane). He had practiced medicine for over fifty years in San Antonio and had retired about three years ago and bought a small ranch outside Bugscuffle and kept a few horses on it. He too was widowed and had moved to North Texas to be near his daughter and granddaughters who lived in Dallas. He became the Club's triple expert - medicine, Mexicans, and the Catholic religion.

Lester ("Pinch") Green - Pinch was called Pinch because he pinched pennies. They joked that he and his brother invented copper wire by fighting over a penny. He was a real tightwad even though everyone knew he had enough money to burn a wet elephant. Lester was a highly educated Easterner who grew up in New York City. He had degrees in accounting, business administration, and economics and had come to Texas years ago to work for one of the large accounting firms in Houston (one of the Arthurs I think). His New York wife divorced him rather than move to Texas. When he got acclimated to Texas he changed his name from Greenfelt and married a rich widow and moved to Fort Worth where he owned and operated a wholesale liquor business, a used furniture store, a scrap yard, and a few other businesses. About three years ago he divorced his wife and escaped to a small ranch he owned near Bugscuffle. In his departure from cowtown he managed to latch on to his 26 year old shapely blonde secretary and brought her with him - so he would have some company as he explained it. Lester was the Club's expert in business, money, economics and shapely blondes.

Cletus ("Professor") Carpenter, PHD. - Cletus retired from teaching school but had held down several government jobs prior to taking up teaching. After he got his PHD in Library Science from TWU he went to work for the Department of Agriculture, then was an aid to a Senator (Yarborough),and next was an IRS agent - then finally a teacher, (then school administrator). He was a lay reader of the Baptist Church and was now living with his fifth wife. They took care of a ranch outside of town for a wealthy insurance executive from Dallas. Cletus was the self proclaimed expert in politics, library science, taxes, religion, and school teaching.

Stewart ("Ace") McGraw - Ace had been an astronaut, test pilot, and finally an executive for a consulting engineering firm (space experts). He held advanced engineering degrees from M.I.T. He had been severely injured in a rocket launching accident and retired early with a fat disability pension as well as a very favorable settlement from litigation (against the government). He had been through three marriages and was now living with the widow Smith on her small horse farm outside town. His expertise was anything mechanical, scientific, or engineering.

Substitutes -

Benjy ("Geek") Green - One of Pinch's sons who visited from time to time. He was a young computer whiz from Dallas. Benjy was single.

Ferlin ("Bulldog") Bucy - Billy Frankel's step son who along with his wife, Gayle, lived with the Frankel's (actually, an upstairs apartment) and ran a convenience store in Bowie.

- CONTENTS -

- CONTENTS - Continued

CHAPTER 1

GETTING ORGANIZED

Bugscuffle wasn't much – just a wide place in a FM (Farm to Market) Road in Jack County North Texas. You might call it a ghost town except for the fact it never was a "Town". The only structure was an old, run down and abandoned filling station.

There was no magnetic attraction in Bugscuffle that I know of and it was just fate that caused all of the brain power to settle in the vicinity. There is no other explanation - or is there?

Judge Abraham (Abe) Handhart bought the land upon which the abandoned filling station stood. He had a nice 3 bedroom brick house built near the lake on the property and had hired a couple of local men to repair the fences and clean up the land. After this was accomplished he mostly "rested" but was getting bored. He bought a few goats to keep the brush under control and put a sign on the front gate - Rocky Mount Goat Ranch.

One day he was puttering around and examined the old building in great detail. He decided that it could be made habitable with a few dollars worth of materials and some labor and sweat. What the heck – why not fix it up and make a little office out of it. So he cranked up the old Ford pickup he had purchased the week before and drove to Jacksboro and bought some roofing, boards, nails, paint, etc.

The next morning he was up with the roosters and starting the "remodeling" project. Before he had completed patching the roof a Dodge Doolie pickup passed and in a couple of minutes it returned and stopped. A tall cowboy looking feller crawled out of the

Doolie, looked up at Abe, and said "Howdy Partner – you gonna open up this filling station". "No" said Abe, "Thought I'd fix it up for my office." "What kind of office?" in quizzed Cowboy. "None of your danged business" responded Abe.

"Bring your sorry butt down off that roof and I'll make it my business, mister." challenged Cowboy. The Judge was already climbing down the ladder trying to decide whether to try to kick that smart cowboy's butt or try to make a friend out of him. He still hadn't decided when he got to the ground and as he turned around, Cowboy was standing (all 6 feet and 7 inches of him) there waiting for him – and that made the decision easy.

Cowboy extended his hand and said "You old fart, you're my kind of man - I'm Billy Frankel and I've got a place up the road a ways. Pass here every day or two and saw when they built your house and had been meaning to stop and meet you. The judge grabbed his hand , squeezed it as hard as he could and pumping it mightily he said "Pleased to meet you Billy - my name is Abe Hardhart and I just bought this place about 3 months ago. I've retired and am going to live here permanent."

Cowboy said "By the way, everybody around here calls me Cowboy. Could you handle a beer?" The judge said "Does a one legged duck swim in a circle? And you can call me Abe." Cowboy chuckled and walked over to his Dodge which he had parked in the shade and removed two ice cold Coors from an ice chest. Abe had followed him to his truck so Cowboy dropped the tail gate and handed Abe a Coors. They sat on the tailgate and sipped beer and visited, each curious about the others history, likes, and dislikes, etc.

Cowboy, said he had been ranching here about fifteen years and that he, his bride, and the widow Smith had been the only folks around Bugscuffle up until a couple of years ago but now a half dozen or so others had bought property and moved into the area.

Abe asked "Why did folks start moving in around here all of a sudden?" Cowboy replied "Big boobs". the judge looked startled so Cowboy quickly explained - "A couple of years ago a well endowed real estate agent from Bowie was over here and she got listings for a bunch of property around here (from the heirs mostly). She then advertised it in the Dallas, Fort Worth, and Houston newspapers - "Say no more" interrupted Abe. "That was Ms. Copeland who sold me this place - a very personable and sweet young lady." "With big boobs" interrupted Cowboy. "No question about that" concluded Abe.

"Have you met most of these folks" asked Abe. "All of them" replied Cowboy "Matter of fact - here comes Tony now" he replied and started waving his arms at the approaching Un-American pickup (a "Nissan). The little truck pulled off the FM Road and parked next to the Doolie and out stepped Antonio (Tony) G. Gomez M.D. Cowboy said "Tony, meet Abe while I get us some more beer. While Cowboy got the beer Tony and Abe struck up an acquaintance. Cowboy rejoined them and Abe asked "What do you all do for entertainment out here?" Tony said "Read and watch T.V." and Cowboy said "Wal - in the spring you can watch tornados; in the summer you can fish and hunt rattlesnakes; in the fall you can bale hay and bird hunt; and in the winter you can sit by the fire and read and watch T.V. or go outside and deer hunt and freeze your tail off." The judge allowed that none of those choices appealed to him with the exception maybe of fishing. Cowboy said "There's 3 lakes and 7 stock tanks on my ranch and each has fish and you are welcome to go fishing in any of them at any time - and so are you Tony.

They sipped on their beers and Cowboy pulled out his can of Copenhagen and took a pinch and offered it to the others - but no takers. He looked at both of them and said "City slickers." Abe pulled out a pouch of chewing tobacco and stuffed a handful in his mouth and offered the pouch to them. Tony said "Think I'll try this" and got a small serving. They continued to sip beer and spit tobacco juice.

After a few moments of silence, Cowboy spoke up "You know, I've been thinking about what you asked - you know, what do you do for entertainment? And I remembered that when old man Orange owned this place and ran the filling station, he had a table and chairs over in the corner and folks used to gather here and play dominos. It was fun. "That's a great idea" said Abe. I remember the country store in Kemp, where I grew up, was where folks congregated and played dominos, whittled on sticks, chewed tobacco and spat, and just visited - that was long before T.V. of course. But probably nobody would be interested in those things anymore." "Aye gad I would" spoke up Cowboy. "Me too" said Tony "Except I don't know how to play dominoes." "<u>Dominos</u>" corrected Cowboy. Tony looked hurt.

"Tell you what" spoke Abe, "Check with other folks around here and if you can come up with three more <u>committed</u> players, I'll re-open this old filling station as a domino parlor. "Deal" echoed Cowboy and Tony. "Assuming we get 3 more, when can we get together and get the show on the road" asked Abe. "Let's meet here next Saturday morning" suggested Cowboy. They agreed and Cowboy and Tony left and Abe got back to his handyman work - except now it had become a mission. He spent the rest of the day patching and painting. He went to bed that night feeling good and got up the next morning early and finished the project. Or so he thought.

Saturday morning rolled around before you knew it and by the time Abe got dressed and finished his coffee; the pickup trucks had already started arriving and assembling by the ex filling station - now domino parlor. Abe walked over and joined them and Cowboy had already taken over and had the ball rolling. When Abe started to say something, Cowboy interrupted and started to introduce the newcomers to Abe in this order - Lester (Pinch) Green, Cletus (Professor) Carpenter, Stewart (Ace) McGraw, Benny (Geek) Green, and last but not least, Ferlin (Bulldog) Bucy, a roly poly 280 pounder.

Cowboy, said "Professor, why don't you read the to-do list and see if Abe wants to add anything." Professor cleared his throat and commenced reading from his list (he had volunteered to be the recording secretary). He read -

(1) Purpose of club - to provide entertainment and recreation for the male members of the Bugscuffle
    Community as well as a forum to discuss and resolve the long range problems of the world.
    (2) Name of the organization - the Bugscuffle Domino, Whittle, and Spit Club.
    (3) Annual dues - $20 in U.S. currency (no checks) - any voluntary contributions also appreciated.
    (4) Board of Directors - All members current with their dues.
    (5) Officers - Just one - the HMFIC (The Head Mother in Charge)
    (6) Things needed to finish out the club house:
        (a) Re wire the place and have Wise county

electric co-op come out and connect the
electricity (and put in a meter).
(b) Put in a new floor
(c) Replace a broken window (and <u>maybe</u>
add curtains)
(d) Put in a refrigerator
(e) Put in a chest of drawers or build shelves
(f) Put in a table and chairs (and maybe a
couch and bench for outside)
(g) Install a wood burning stove
(h) Install window air conditioner
(i) Improve the lighting somehow
(7) Other stuff to do
(a) Write <u>official</u> rules to govern domino
playing and any gambling that might
accompany play
(b) Get some beer and water
(c) Get a tablet (to keep score)
(d) Get a coffee pot - and coffee
(e) Get a big bottle of aspirin
(f) Get a case of vienna sausages and a box
of soda crackers (for snacks) - and a jar
of peanut butter - and some cheese whiz -
and paper plates and plastic spoons
(8) Rules and other sources of revenue
(a) The rest room doesn't work so the door
has been nailed shut. If you need to
bleed your lizard, just step out back and
cut loose. If you need to do no. 2, it will
cost you $5 a trip to use Abe's bath room
- or you can go home and do it for free
(b) No farting - Each time you fart it will cost

you $3 - $5 if it is extra loud or odorous.

(c) No cheating - If you are caught cheating it will cost you $50 - No exceptions!!

(d) 10% of <u>every</u> gambling pot goes to the club treasury

(e) No women - period. Anyone bringing a female to any session without prior approval by the board will be automatically <u>expelled</u>.

(f) No smoking inside - go outside to smoke. Chewing or dipping is ok inside so long a as you use a spittoon. No spiting on the floor.

Abe had listened intently and smiled a couple of times as things were read. As Cletus finished Cowboy said "Abe, did we miss anything?" Abe said, First, don't worry about the wiring or electricity, I've got a man coming out Monday to take care of that, also, you will note that I have placed a latch and combination lock on the door. It is a tumbler lock and the combination is 1,2,3,4. Everyone is welcome to open up and come in as they please. Remember - 1,2,3,4. (Out of the corner of his eye he saw Professor writing it down on his list.)

Cowboy said "Since Abe is taking care of the major item on the list - do I have any volunteers for the other items - Professor take notes." Ace spoke first and said "I have a practically new refrigerator that I'll contribute if some of you will help me load it." Bulldog said "I'll go get it right after this meeting - I've got my pickup parked outside (as did everyone else) Ace "I've also got a microwave oven if you need it too." "Bring it" said Cowboy.

Cowboy spoke again and said to Bulldog "I just remember - there's an old cast iron wood burning stove in the barn - bring it down here too. It's got 4 cracks in it but you can get some JB Weld and patch it up when you get the chimney and install it."

Pinch spoke up - "I can't remember everything on the list but I've got connections in Fort Worth and can get just about anything wholesale - please read the items and mark me down for what I tell you - then make me a list of what I offered. The Professor started down the list and marked Pinch down for 6(a),(f) & (h) and 7(d). As he read the list others volunteered, as follows:

6 (b) - Tony Gomez
6 (c) - Tony Gomez
6 (i) - Tony Gomez

Tony said he had a carpenter doing some remodeling at his place and he would bring him down to take care of these items - except the curtains. Cowboy spoke up - "Aw heck, I'll have Lucy make some curtains". "And by the way, I'll also get Lucy to help me write the rules - which we'll vote on before they become official - and I'm going to Munster tonight to get my month's supply of

14

beer so I'll bring a couple of cases and drop them off here.

The professor said, "That takes care of everything on the list except 6(b) - water, 6(c) tablet 6(d) coffee 6(f) vienna's, crackers, peanut butter, and cheese whiz. "Stop right there. "said Bulldog," Heck, I run a grocery store and if you'll give me a list I'll bring all that stuff".

The Professor said "Last item dominos" - and I'll take care of them."

Cowboy said "Last item of business - election of officers - I nominate Abe." Pinch said "I second" and Tony added "I propose that nominations be closed - all in favor say aye" aye, aye, aye, "opposed" Abe said - guess I'm it then. Everyone responded <u>AYE!</u>

"Meeting adjourned, see you all next Saturday morning "said Abe and everyone departed. And that, dear Heart , is how the Bugscuffle Domino, Whittle and Spit Club was born.

CHAPTER 2

MONEY TALKS AND

BULLPOOP WALKS

The following Saturday morning everyone (except Bulldog) gathered at the remodeled club house. The spent a few minutes inspecting all the changes which had been made since last Saturday. The table and chairs were a dinette set (in top shape) and the refrigeration was practically new. The stove had been patched so you could hardly find where the crack had been – and it had been painted so it at least looked new (liquid overhaul) and the lighting was excellent – fluorescent no less. The floor was rough hardwood and Tony said he was going to get some linoleum or tiles to cover it. Everyone was opposed to that idea – they said leave it just like it is – we won't feel bad about tracking mud in here when it rains. "Ok".

Abe made a pot of coffee and after it brewed everyone got a Styrofoam cup and started sipping. Tony complained because there was no cream, sugar, or sweet-n-low. "Sissy" said Ace.

Cowboy announced, "You all take a seat and let's get a few things out of the way before we shuffle the ivories." When everyone was seated and settled down, Cowboy handed out the Rules (and instructions) that he and Lucy had prepared.

They spent a few minutes reading them, then Cowboy asked "Any questions?" Ace said "No question - I just don't like that last item - no smoking inside." Pinch said "Me either". Cowboy said "I really don't either - shall we change it to - smoking allowed?" Everyone responded

"Yeah." Do you approve the rules now - raise your hand for yes. Everyone raised their hand - rules now in force.

Cowboy then handed everyone a copy of the rules and a copy of instructions for playing dominos - as follows:

Domino's

How the Game(s) Are Played (The Rules)

Background

Dominos are one of the oldest games known to mankind and have been tracked back as far as the Ming dynasty (China – Circa 1400). There is no record as to the beginning of game but it appears the credit belongs to some old, old, Chinaman. The domino has been made from wood, clay, elephant tusk, and today – plastic. A domino is rectangular shaped and contains dots (representing numbers) on one face and a design on the other side. The numbers range from <u>none</u> (blanks) to six. The side with the dots is bi-sected and dots appear on each side (half). There are <u>28</u> dominos in a set. (illustrated):

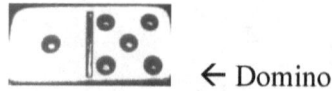 ← Domino

Domino Set ----

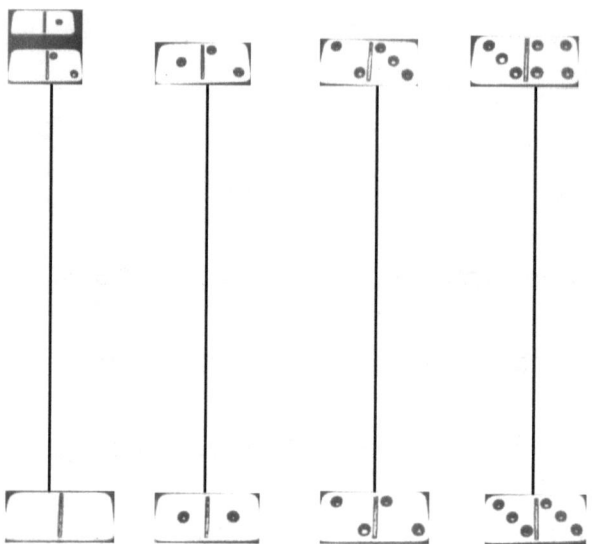

7 blanks   6 ones   5 two's   4 three's

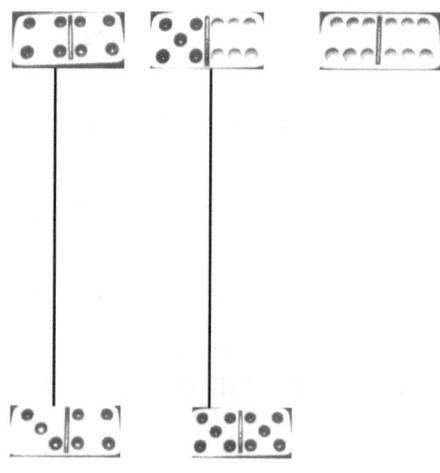

3 fours   fives   1 six

Domino Games

There are several games you can play with these little "Ivories" but the two most popular are:

(A) Just Plain Ole Dominos

The object of this game is to get rid of the dominos in your hand as quickly as possible and try to score points as you lay down each domino. Points are scored when the aggregate count of all <u>end</u> halves of the face up dominos on the board (table) is divisible by <u>5</u>. When the first player has used up all the dominos in his hands, the point count of dominos remaining in the other players hands are <u>subtracted</u> from their score.

(We'll go through a couple of actual games in detail later in this book to illustrate).

(B) Forty – two (sometimes called "Moon")

The object of this game is to score points by capturing "Tricks". IT is similar to several card games including spades, hearts, and bridge. Normally, there are forty two points possible with each hand (with the standard 4 players) 7 for tricks, two ten's, and three fives. All the dominos are placed face down on the table and the "dealer" scrambles them up by moving them around. (Everyone develops their own style of mixing). Each player picks 7 dominos for his "Hand".

The bidding starts with the player to the left of the dealer and goes clockwise around the table. If everyone passes – the dealer is stuck with a 21 bid.

The high bidder names trumps – for example – threes.

If you are playing "partners", partners (with the bid) exchange two dominos (by sliding them across the table face down).

Play begins with the high bidder playing the first domino – normally his highest trump. Everyone plays following clockwise around the table and is required to follow suit.

(Here again – read on for a couple of games described in detail).

Betting – maximum bet is 1¢ per point. A running score will be kept and all bets must be settled on the first meeting of each month. Then the slate is wiped clean and we start all over.

"Any questions" asked Cowboy "Yes" said Cletus the "Professor" – I don't understand the betting part – especially how you "settle up." "Good point" answered

Billy. "It's sort of like a rodeo event on a golf tournament – winner takes all. For example if at the first meeting next month our points were accumulated and Abe has 250 points – 42 more than the next man which is me with 208 points. Then <u>everyone</u> must pay Abe two dollars and fifty cents (250 pennies).

"Any more questions"? - Silence -------fine, let's run through a hand of each game to illustrate how you play. "Where are the dominos?" "They're out in my truck" answered Professor – I'll go get them. He returned in a couple of minutes and dropped a small plastic bag with Wally World (Wal-mart) on it. Cowboy picked it up and removed the box of dominos and dumped them on the table. He threw the box and plastic bag on the floor. (Tony made a mental note – need a trash can). Abe spat tobacco juice on the floor. (Tony added to his mental note – also a spittoon)

Cowboy proceeded to flip the dominos over so no "spots" were showing. One by one the others pitched in and when only the backs were showing, Billy placed both hands palm down and started scrambling the dominos by moving his hands in circular motions. When he had finished he said "Now we are going to play a round of plain ole dominos." Professor, get that legal pad and write everyone's name over a column and you can keep score. Professor complied with the request (order).

Cowboy asked "Anyone remember how many dominos there are in a set." "Twenty eight" responded Ace. "That's right" came back Cowboy "How many times will six go into twenty eight?" "4.67" shot back Ace "I ain't that good in mental math" responded Cowboy "But it don't make no differences – we ain't going to start sawing up these new dominos no how "Everybody take four dominos and put them edge ways down so they can see the spots – the four left over are going to be four "draws" – we call them the "Kitty."

The players were seated clockwise around the table, starting with Cowboy in this order – Ace, Abe, Professor, Pinch, and Tony. Cowboy said, "Remember, you get points when the aggregate end numbers are divisible by five ." "Who has the spinner?" No response – confused looks only. "The spinner is the <u>double six</u>." "I do "said Pinch who laid it down. "Now Tony – you can play a six on either side or end of that double six". – The best play would be a six, three on the side ." Tony said." The only six I have is a six/one" so he placed it on the side. "Now it's my turn and I'm going to pick up fifteen points" said

Cowboy as he played the one/three. The dominos were now in this order.

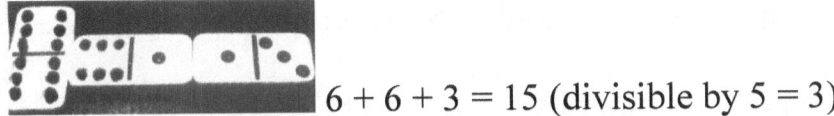 $6 + 6 + 3 = 15$ (divisible by $5 = 3$)

All their faces lit up as the simplicity of the game became obvious. Ace was grinning like a possum eating persimmons as he placed the six/five opposite the six/one – "Twenty points? He annoyance. $(6 + 6 + 3 + 5 = 20)$. "You got that right Ace "agreed Cowboy "Your play Abe." Abe seemed confused. He finally said "I don't have anything with a six on it." Cowboy patiently answered "You can also play a three or five – got either of them." "Yes but I'm not sure which is the best". Meekly responded Abe. Cowboy said "Let me look at your hand" and he got up and walked around behind Abe and looked at his dominos for an instant before he blurted out "Gee, you don't have to be a rocket scientist to see 25 points – play the double five." Ace, who was in fact a rocket scientist, gave Cowboy a very vindictive look as Abe laid down the double five and quietly said "Twenty five points, by golly", (6 + 6 + 3 + 5 + 5 = 25) Abe announced "And twenty five more "as he laid down the five/blank. Cowboy said "Take that one back - - not your turn".

The board now looked like this:

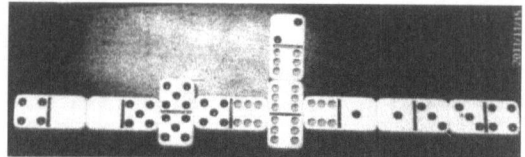

(1) Professor next played a three-four for no count. (2) then Pinch thrumphrtly slapped down the four-blank for 30 points and smiled knowingly at Cowboy, Tony quickly played the six/two and again no count. Then it was Cowboy's turn again and he said "Time for the next

lesson – I don't have a 4,5 or 6 in my hand – so I have to draw out of the Kitty. He took one domino from the 4 on the table and frowned – "Doggone he said "This one won't play either so he took another one and played it on the five – it was the five/one – no count though. Ace next played the one/four and said "Mark me down   for 30 points Professor ole buddy." He lit a cigarette and leaned back in his chair and said "Tony, would you please reach into the refrigerator and hand me a beer." Tony said "Sure – anyone else?" Pinch said

   "Let's take five." So they got up, stretched, and started popping beer tops and discussing the domino "lesson". Cowboy was eaves dropping and it became obvious to him that everyone in the group had learned the basic game of dominos.

Out of the clear blue, Professor raised the question of the day – "Why do folks act like they act? I mean, what drives most decisions?"

"That's easy" spoke up Pinch "Money". "In my opinion, about 99% of all human decisions and actions are dollar decisions." If you can track the dollars you can get to the bottom (truth) of anything." "What about chasing poon tang" inquired Ace. "That's the other 1%" replied Pinch.

There's an expression in the country "Money talks and bullpoop walks" spoke up Cowboy. I guess I would have to agree with you. "Studying about it - I can't think of hardly any decisions I make that I don't first figure either how much I can make or how much it is going to cost me. What do you think Abe?"

The judge took a long ,slow swig of beer; took out his pipe, filled and lit it and said "In my career I made thousands of decisions but most of them were interpreting the law's of the land and were not, therefore, money driven." "Maybe not, technically," agreed Pinch "But the law itself was based on economic or dollar decisions."

"But money is the root of all evil" said Professor. "Says who?" demanded Tony. "The good book – the Bible" replied Professor. "Not true countered Tony, In the Fourth Chapter of Mark, verse 16, it is written "For the <u>love</u> of money is at the root of all evil. I think that means that if anyone becomes obsessed with only money – that is where the evil comes in." "I concur" spoke up Abe, and most of the others nodded in agreement.

By now it was almost 1pm and everyone was starting to get hungry. The mice had gnawed into the cracker box and no one would touch the crackers.

Billy asked "You all want to finish the domino game – or what?" Ace said "I've got to be going – I promised madam (widow Smith) that I would drive her up to Wichita Falls this afternoon. Cletus followed with "I've got about the same problems – my wife has some things she wants me to do this afternoon."

Pinch announced "Think I'll drive over to the Green Frog in Jacksboro for lunch – anyone interested?" They all were. Lester said "All four of us won't fit comfortably in any pickup so why don't you boys follow me home and we'll get my car to drive to town. Everyone nodded ok (yes) and got into their trucks and formed up the caravan. It was less than a mile to Pinch's place. He parked his truck under a tree and walked over to his garage, punched a button, and the door started to open. He entered the garage and in moments backed out a silver and black Rolls Royce. "Dad gum" said Cowboy "That's the first one of them things I ever saw = much less rode in".

They loaded up and headed to Jacksboro in style.

CHAPTER 3

CRIME AND PUNISHMENT

While they were traveling they discussed "reasons" for things and Pinch had said all decisions were dollar based. Before anyone countered they had reached Jacksboro.

They pulled up in front of the Green Frog and parked and went inside. The restaurant was deserted and the waitress led them to a large table in the smoking section. They sat down and she took their iced tea orders. In a moment she returned with giant sized glasses of iced tea and four menus which she distributed. "Where's everybody at?" Inquired Cowboy." "I guess shopping or home watching a ball game or messing around" responded the skinny blonde "It is 3pm on a Saturday afternoon you know." "Didn't realize it was that late" said Tony. "I sure as heck did" Cut in Abe, "My stomach thinks my throats been cut."

"Ready to order?" Inquired the blonde. "Yep – bring me some mountain oysters, hash browns, and a salt with ranch" responded Cowboy. "What are mountain oysters?" Asked Pinch. "Calf balls" responded the blonde and everyone (except Lester) laughed. Lester blushed and said "I'll try the catfish with hash browns and a Caesar salad." Tony was looking at the lunch menu and said "I'll have the lunch special – the meat loaf with green beans and mashed potatoes". The waitress said "I don't think there is any meat loaf left – let me go check."

While she was gone Abe asked Cowboy "Are those calf balls any good – I've never tried them." Cowboy said "I love em." The judge commented "That's a purty good looking gal – for an older woman – she must be about 60." When the waitress returned she said "Meat loaf's gone but we still have a few stuffed pork chops (day old). Tony said "Pork chops then." Everyone's attention focused on Abe. He finally said "Young lady, there's three things I've never tried in my life and I think I'll try two of them right now." "Bring me some frog legs, calf balls, hash browns, and cole slaw." She smiled and asked "And the third thing? He said "I'll tell you later." She gave him another knowing smile and left to turn in their orders.

Cowboy laughed and said "Judge, I believe you could get a little of that if you tried hard." The other two couldn't believe what they had heard and were mortified when the judge responded "Think I'll give it a try – if the mountain oysters work like real oysters." "If they don't,

I've got a bottle of Viagra in my truck that you can have, "volunteered Tony.

The waitress brought their food and it was delicious as food usually is if you are extremely hungry. Tony and Pinch even tried a taste of the mountain oysters. After they finished eating and fired up their smokes, Pinch said "All you hear on T.V. or read in the paper these days is rape, robbery, murder, child molestation, and whatever other crimes you can think of - how are we even going to get crime and criminals under control?"

"I think we should use more psychiatrist and give prisoners more psychiatric treatment when they are in prison" said Tony (himself a medical doctor). "That don't work" cut in Cowboy "We need to hang more of the sons of bitches – ain't that right Judge?

Abe sat there for a while before he said "Boys, I've spent my entire life wrestling with the problem and I've never told anyone what I'm about to tell you – most would think I was a crazy radical – and you may also but I'll tell you anyway."

"Do you remember what Pinch said, this very morning, that all (or virtually all) decisions were based on economics." They nodded and he continued – "Well I believe the solution to crime is also an economic solution – applied somewhat as follows."

"Fundamentally, we would place a dollar value on each criminal act – i.e. a crime price list. A convicted criminal would become a "slave" and be forced to "work out" the price of the crime he committed, a major portion of the dollars he worked out would be given to the victims of his crime - the balance would pay for his upkeep or placed in a crime "pool. After he repaid his criminal debt he could re join society – under certain conditions. Does everyone grasp the concept"?"

"By gosh I think you have the answer" said Cowboy. "I can see lots of problems in developing the price lists as well as decided how the prisoners are to earn the money and how the money is to be divided" said Pinch. "Yes, and the certain conditions gives me problems" added Tony.

"All of your concerns and questions are quite valid" said the Judge. "Admittedly, this is not a perfect solutions and there are numerous details to be worked out – However, I believe it is worth a try and I firmly believe crime would be drastically reduced and society would benefit immensely from this system".

"This is very thought provoking stuff" said Pinch. "Maybe we could develop it further and present it to our senator or something." "Yes, go into the details further" begged Cowboy. "I'm not sure I want to hear this "added Tony. "Don't be a chicken Tony" cautioned Cowboy.

"Very well" answered Abe. "We can discuss the following categories and I think you will begin to understand the problems yet to be resolved.

"First, let's discuss the crime price list. We will start with the easier items" Crimes involving the theft of property or destruction of property are not that difficult. For example, if an arsonist burned down a warehouse buildings containing inventory items we could develop the <u>price</u> of his crime somewhat as follows –

1. Building value – appraised value or depreciated

   cost   say $ 800,000

2. Contents value – cost basis of the stored

   inventory   say   263,000

           Total $1,063,000

Or, let's say a thief stole a T.V. set from a residence

and sold it to a stranger – not able to trace or recover.

           Replacement cost of T.V. set $ 1,050

Or, a thief stole a car and wrecked it.

           Replacement cost of car $18,500

All of these crimes involving property become a matter

of establishing a "Fair Value" of the property involved.

And this "Fair Value" can be reasonable established.

The next category involves <u>damage</u> to human beings and here we have problems. The most serious problem is that of establishing the <u>value</u> of a human life. I have concluded that the only solution in this area of setting or determines value is purely arbitrarily. For example –

<u>Human Life Values</u>:

<u>Age</u>	<u>Male</u>	<u>Female</u>
Over 65	$ 500,000	$ 400,000
50-65	600,000	450,000
40-50	700,000	550,000
30-40	800,000	650,000
20-30	900,000	750,000
Under 20	1,000,000	850,000

Loss of limbs, etc. – use insurance claim and settlement information.

Next, we must decide how the criminals are to earn the money – and where. Further, how much should they be paid.

Again, let's start with the easier question – where? We must use our present prison facilities – for economic reasons. However, we could eliminate the state facilities and treat those crimes as <u>Federal</u>. This alone would save millions, billions, even zillions!!! We would leave the local system in place for traffic fines, etc.

Each prison would become a farm, factory, or both.

The farms would produce food products – to be sold on world markets.

The factories would produce stuff that we have lost to cheap labor in third world countries. Any other nasty jobs that no one else wants to do – i.e., garbage collection.

The prisoners would be paid the minimum wage with <u>no</u> fringe benefits – except for maybe <u>basic</u> health benefits.

An amount would be deducted from each pay check to take care of their upkeep. – Say $15.00 per day.

Finally – under what terms would the prisoners be put back into society.

My suggestion would be –

1. Murders – <u>Never</u> – Go ahead and execute them after they pay the dollar debt.

2. Rapist – Castrate them, brand "R" on their forehead – then release.

3. Child molesters – Same as rapist except change the brand to C.M.

4. Any second offender – Brand a <u>2</u> on their forehead.

5. Anyone who has been convicted more than 5 times – never – just keep them working and putting their wages in the Kitty.

Let's look at a couple of examples:

(A)   Joe Blow robs a convenience store and get away with $5,000. He is captured and convicted and none of the money is recovered.

Joe is sent to a prison that has an agriculture facility that raises potatoes.

He works for 140 days and is released. The money he earns is distributed as follows:

Joe works (140 x 8)   1120 hours

Joe earns (1120 x 6.50) $7,800

Joe earnings are distributed as follows:

*Convenience store	$5,000
*Prison (15 x 140)	2,100
*To Joe when he is released	700
Total	$7,800

Tony said "I still don't think it would work." But Cowboy said, even more enthusiastically than before. "I darn sure think it would and I'd vote for it in a New York minute – but first I got to go pee." Tony said "Me too" Pinch added "Me three" and they headed for the restroom.

As soon as the three disappeared into the restroom Abe motioned for the waitress. She sprinted over and said "I left your check on the table – did I forget something?"

The Abe smiled and said "Yep, I didn't get your name or phone number." She said "I'll swap with you" and tore a blank two tickets from her ticket book and gave Abe one. She sat down at the table and printed the info on the other and handed it to the judge. He removed a business card from his wallet and handed it to her. The information exchanged was:

Her printed info:

Margie Lee Rouch
216 Decatur St., Apt 115
Jacksonsboro, Texas 76266
949-816-xxxx

His business card info:

Abe Hardhart
Rocky Mount Goat Ranch
Bugscuffle, Texas 76270
949-777-xxxx (Ranch)
922-819-xxxx (Mobil)

She asked "Do you raise goats?" He said "Yep". Her next questions "Are you retired?" "Yep" – and "What did you use to do?" "Judge" he responded. And finally "What was that third thing?" He grinned and said "Seduce a blonde till she hollered "Enough!" Then he asked "How about a date tonight?" She said "Ok – pick me up at 7:00 pm." He said "I'll be there."

Cowboy and Tony returned as Margie was leaving. Cowboy asked "What were you all talking about?" And the judge replied "goats." They got up to leave and Abe left a $20 tip and Pinch paid the bill. They got into his Rolls Royce and headed back to Bugscuffle. All Abe thought of on the drive was "I'm back in the saddle again. (Maybe)".

CHAPTER 4

ENOUGH! STOP! STOP! – DON'T STOP......

When they pulled into Pinch's place and unloaded, Abe tugged at Tonys sleeve and motioned him aside. Tony asked "What's wrong?" Abe said "If you were serious about them pills – I'll take you up on your offer." Tony thought for a minute then smiled and said "Sure – come on over to my truck and I'll get them for you." Abe followed him to his Nissan and waited until tony probed around the glove compartment and came up with a sample pack of Viagra which he handed to Abe.

Abe examined the pack for a minute and asked "How much do I owe you? Do you take all six pills at one time?" Tony replied "No charge – that is a sample pack that the drug company gives to doctors." "And <u>read</u> the instructions – those pills could kill you if you have heart problems (they got Sinatra they say) – take <u>one</u> an hour before you try to perform." Abe had put on his glasses. And he already decided to experiment with one pill <u>before</u> his hot date with Margie. "Thanks Tony – I owe you" he said and then got into his old Dodge pickup and heady for his Rocky Mountain Goat Ranch.

It was almost 4pm when Abe got to the house. All he had been thinking about since exchanging info with Margie was Margie, the pills, and related matters. He got a knife out of the drawer and punctured the packages and took out one of the little pale blue, greekish looking pills and examined it. Then he got a glass of water and took the medicine. He went to the bedroom and set the alarm clock for 5:30 and took off his clothes and lay down for a nap. If things worked out as he planned he would need all his strength around dark thirty. Soon he dozed off.

Buzz! Buzz! Buzz! The alarm sounded. Abe rolled over to turn off the alarm and made an amazing discovery. His old tool was swollen up larger than it had been in years and was so stiff and hard that a cat couldn't scratch it. "Dang" he muttered to himself – that little pill does work." He almost masturbated but thought "Naw – I'll save it for Margie – I think she is looking forward to it as much as me." He took a shower instead, shaved, and got dressed. Somewhere in the process his tool had shrunk back to normal. He put on some expensive cologne, put his cell phone in his pocket , and walked to his Cadillac and got in. He started it and backed out of the garage.

He headed toward Jacksboro and when he got to the edge of town he pulled into a Phillips 66 station (actually an Allsups), filled up with gas, and got directions to

Decatur Street. He also got directions to a flower and gift shop and swung by it and got a vase of 6 roses. He parked in front of Margie's apartment, got out, and rang her door bell. She came to the door and opened it and invited him inside. He said "My, you sure look nice" and she responded "You do too - and smell good." He handed her the roses and she got teary eyed and said "That's the first time a man has given me flowers in years" and gave him a big kiss. Abe almost shook with excitement and anticipation.

Abe sat down on the couch and Margie took her roses and put them in the refrigerator. she sat down beside him and asked "What are we going to do?" Abe's eyes were focused on her ample boobs which were prominently displayed by the tight fitting knit dress she wore - and she added "Besides that? Abe said "I'm sort of new around these parts and open to suggestions - Do you want to go eat? Is there a movie in town? Anything else going on?"

Margie said "I'm around food all day so eating doesn't appeal to me - maybe later." I got a paper and there's a movie over at the theater in Graham that I'd like to see - Titanic." Abe said "Let's go" and they got up and left. On the short drive to Graham each gave the other a "capsule life story".

Abe told her that he was a lawyer and a retired judge. He told her of the death of his wife about seven years ago and that he had not been with another woman since. He said he had two grown children - a son (also a lawyer) who was with a big law firm in Houston, and a daughter who was a school teacher in Baton Rouge, Louisiana. Both were married and he had five grandchildren.

Margie said she was still legally married she guessed - but her worthless husband (an oil field roughneck, drunkard, and gambler) had abandoned her about four years ago and she had no idea as to his whereabouts. The last word she had - he was in Alaska. She had a daughter in Fort Worth who was divorced and raising two little boys. She had worked for a telecom company in Fort Worth up until a year ago and had been laid off. Her good friend Carla, who lived in the same apartment had got her the job at the Green Frog and she had moved to Jacksboro. She admitted that she had had a couple of dates but the men were so crude that she quit going out.

When they got to the theater, the movie had already started but they went in anyway, by the time they were seated the Titanic had already struck the iceberg and was starting to list. They snuggled closer and held hands. By the time the movie was over, they were smooching and he was rubbing her thigh. They left the theater and go into his Cadillac and Abe asked "Where to - ready to go eat?" Margie responded "Why don't we go back to my place - we can stop at the Taco Bell and get some tacos and cokes and take them with us." Abe thought that was an excellent idea - and said so.

They went into her apartment and took the tacos and cokes to her kitchen and sat at the table and ate. Abe secretly removed one of the Viagra pills and swallowed it while they were eating. When they had finished they retired to the couch and Margie turned on the T.V. and handed the control to Abe and said "Take off your boots and tie and relax while I go slip into something more comfortable." She went into the bedroom and he started searching through the channels - finally he located a movie that looked like it might have some romance in it and left it on. Margie returned, clad in a pink robe and fluffy pink house slippers and sat down next to him.

He put his arm around her and pulled her closer and kissed her on the neck and ear. She sat us and said "What kind of a girl do you think I am - the loose kind that kisses and fools around on the first date?" "Oh heck no" soothed Abe. "But, let's be realistic - we are both getting on in years and have been there and done that - we're both lonely and, I think, need each other and are attracted to each other - and I also think we should take advantage of this opportunity. Heck, I might have a heart attack or something tomorrow - and die; if I did would you be sorry we didn't make love - even if it is our first date?" She thought about it for a few minutes and finally said "You may be right" and she placed her lips on his and they kissed passionately. One thing led to another and they soon moved to her bedroom for a romantic encounter when they finished he looked at the luminous dial on her clock on the bed stand - Ye gads - 3:00 a.m. he said "I'd better go" and got up. She got up too and begged him to stay. He was set on leaving so they took a shower together and he got dressed and drove home. He knew that he had to have some more of that good stuff - but he didn't think it was worth marrying for. But still - it sure was good and he felt great.

Margie went back to bed and went to sleep - hearing wedding bells.......

CHAPTER 5

THE GOLDEN RULE – NAW, JUST THE RULE

The boys had gathered on a Blustery winter morning and Abe got there early and built a fire in the pot bellied stove and made the coffee. Geek had brought a sack full of banana nut muffins that he had made. They sat around munching muffins and drinking coffee and Bulldog posted the question "What is the most important factor that dominations our lives?"

Cowboy said "Sex" and Professor said "The Christian way" and Ace said "Survival". They started to argue the point and Pinch interrupted and said "Boys – all of you are wrong although there is some merit to each of your answers. The real answer is "The Almighty Dollar". I told you that last week.

Pinch explained. "There are exceptions to most rules but I think I can demonstrate to you that <u>substantially</u> all decisions are based on the dollar effect (called economics) rather than argue the point – I'll forego a long winded explanation this morning but point out in future discussions where the <u>economic</u> or dollar effect dictates. Fair enough?"

Ace asked "Suppose I had Sadie Blackbush all alone in a motel room and she was drinking with me. We get to follin around and I finally asked her "Do you want to have sex?" Tell me how economics is going to influence her decision?

Pinch said "Knowing Sadie as I do, she would answer "No" and knowing you as I do, you would next say "I'll give you $100 for a little sex." And that's <u>dollars</u> effect. If you really analyze any answer to a question on basis of a decision you will finally realize it was based on money

– pure and simple.

CHAPTER 6

DOCTORING AND MEDICINE

Cowboy's phone rang off the hook on Tuesday. He was out working so everyone got to talk to his recorder. They all wanted to know when the next domino game would take place. So Tuesday night he returned the calls and issued his edict. During the warm months - April through October, the club would meet for dominos and discussion each Saturday morning at 8:00 a.m. During the other months, November through March, they would meet on Wednesday mornings at 9:00 a.m. and on Saturday mornings at 10:00 a.m. Some wanted to meet more often but he hushed them up by telling them, in effect, that he was in charge and those were the rules.

The following Saturday, everyone except Pinch Green was at the "Club House" at 10:00 a.m. Cowboy announced that they would play 42 (or Moon) today. And they would play with partners. He got out the domino's and shuffled them on the table top. Next, he instructed everyone to pick a domino and the two highest would be partners and the two lowest would be partners. The domino's drawn were as follows:

Abe - The six/three
Cowboy - The four/two
Professor - The six/four
Ace - The double four
Tony - The four/one

Billy said - "Abe and Cletus are partners and me and Tony are partners," "Ace if Pinch shows up - you and him are partners, Ok".

Then Cowboy re-shuffled the dominos and told everyone to pick seven dominos and look at them - but don't let anyone else see them. They did as instructed.

He then explained the <u>basics</u> of the game:

Object - to get 42 points before the other side does-

Scoring - one point per trick taken (max 7 points), plus face points for all domino's divisible by five. For example

- three/two - 5 points

- four/one - 5 points

- five/black - 5 points

- five/five - 10 points

- Six/four - 10 points

Total points per hand = 42 points

Bidding - bid the number of points you think you can make. High bidder names trump. (number or doubles) if you don't make your bid you go "set" and the bid is subtracted from your score. Can only bid once.

Passing - After the bidding, high bidder exchanges two dominos with his partner.

First play - high bidder plays first - all must follow suit
- can only <u>trump</u> if you are void in the number lead.

Billy said - "Everybody lay your dominos down on the
table - face up - and we'll walk through a hand. The
following "hands" had been drawn.

Billy - 6/4; 6/3; 5/2; 4/0; 3/3; 3/0; 2/1
Abe - 6/6; 6/5; 5/5; 5/1; 2/2; 2/0; 0/0
Tony -6/0; 5/3; 5/4; 5/0; 4/3; 3/1; 1/0
Professor 6/2; 6/1; 4/4; 4/2; 4/1; 3/2; 1/1

Billy said - Abe could bid about 29 on his hand and
name 6's trump.

Tony would pass; Professor would pass; and I would
be tempted to bid 30 or 31 (on my 3's) but would
probably pass, let's say Abe got the bid at 29 and named
the six trump. He would give his 2/0 and 0/0 to Professor
and Professor would give him the two trump - 6/1 and
6/2.

The play would go as follows -

Caught by		Count
Trick 1 - 6/6; 6/0; 4/1; and 6/3	Abe	6
Trick 2 - 6/5; 1/0; 3/2; and 6/4	Abe	16
Trick 3 - 5/5; 5/3; 2/0; and 5/2	Abe	11
Trick 4 - 5/1; 5/4; 2/1; and 4/0	Tony	1
Trick 5 - 5/2; 4/4; 5/2; and 6/1	Abe	6
Trick 6 - 6/2; 3/1; 4/1; and 4/7	Abe	1
Trick 7 - 2/2	Abe	1

In that example, Abe and Cletus scores 41 and Tony and myself only scored 1. but - beware - it depends on where the dominos fall. The old 6/4 or 5/5 can ruin you - so be careful on bidding. Professor snickered and Cowboy asked "What the heck is so funny?" Professor said "I got a book on dominos and made copies of pertinent sections for everyone and Tony got a bunch of information on the internet which he copied for everyone - we've been studying dominos while you were bailing hay." "Ok, by dang, your shuffle Abe - let's play and see how much you fellers have learned." Cowboy answered.

They played four hands and the score was almost even - they had been studying. They took a break and Professor looked at Tony and asked "Heard you went to Galveston last week - anything special." Tony beamed as he said "Yes, I attended graduation for my son - he got his degree in medicine from UT Med School. He's going to intern in internal medicine at Mercy General Hospital, Denver, Colorado."

Cowboy observed "Why would anyone want to be a doctor anymore - that has gotten to be one of the most screwed up professions there is." The government, Medicare, insurance companies, pharmaceutical companies, and health care providers (What the heck ever they are) have things so screwed up that God and six of his best helpers couldn't straighten it out. And the AMA doesn't help matters either."

Tony became very defensive and said "Medicine is a very noble and gratifying profession - it is very satisfying to help your fellow man when he is sick and in need of care." Cowboy blurted out "Horse crap!" "Does everyone feel (about medicine) like this redneck? Asked Tony.

Abe said "Wal yes, it is screwed up but not any more than anything else these days - practically everything is a screwed up mess these days - and I blame most of it on the Gol darn lawyers." Pinch injected "In that most politicians are, in fact, lawyers, I would agree with Abe up to a point - but I still believe that money is at the

68

bottom of most of it." "When did you come in Pinch?"
Asked Cowboy. Pinch said "About ten minutes ago -
you boys were so engrossed in dominos that I didn't want
to bother you." "What do you have to say Professor?
Pinch asked as he looked Professor in the eye.

Professor thought for a minute before he replied "If
today is the day we straighten out the medical profession
I'll begin with my thoughts on the subject. In summary,
I'll discuss the following:

(a) Shortage of qualified doctors (and nurses) and
some of the reasons why.
(b) Movement toward socialized medicine.
(c) Ridiculous cost of patient treatment and care.
(d) The strangle hold on medicine by the giant
pharmaceutical companies   .
(e) Closed doors and closed minds in medical research
(f) Unbelievable cost of medical equipment.
(g) Malpractice lawsuits and resultant extremely high
cost of insurance.

You can blame the baby boomers for the shortage of
doctors and nurses. In 1965 the Federal government

began subsidized medical residences through Medicare. In the 1970's, congress approved funds for additional places and the boomers flooded into medicine and now represent one third of the establishment. Now they are starting to retire.

At the same time, consumer demand has increased as the entire population grows older. Older people require more health care. Therefore, it will take more doctors to handle the same number of patients. The demand for doctors and nurses by 2020 will be many tens of thousands more than we will have.   We are steadily moving toward socialized medicine - that is, a health system in which the government operates the production of health care and provides its financing. It already exists in the United Kingdom, Canada, Australia, and Russia - just to name a few.

The cost of health care continues to rise - despite government involvement through Medicare, etc.

There is no doubt the giant pharmaceutical companies control medicine - especially its price. They have one of the strongest lobbies in Washington.

Because of the pharmaceutical companies control, substantially all research is in chemistry (i.e. drugs). Very little is done in other areas. And we can't even stop the common cold.

Did you ever think we might use mechanical and/or electronics for cures, makes sense to me.

And newly created medical equipment cost hundreds of thousands - if not millions.

Finally, malpractice lawsuits have gotten out of hand and add billions to the cost of medicine.

"Well Professor - where do we go from here?" Asked Pinch.

"Socialized medicine - no doubt" answered the Professor.

While the professions was talking, Tony was nodding in agreement.

CHAPTER 7

HOW ABOUT THEM COWBOYS?

It was the middle of September and pro-football was just getting into full swing. Except for those drawing byes, all the teams had played two regular season games. For the third season in a row the Dallas Cowboys had jumped off to a 2-0 start. Two losses and zero wins!

Just a few years earlier, all of the group had been avid and quite vocal Cowboy supporters - but not anymore. For the most part they had become "Jerry critics."

Cowboy started the session with his assessment of the current Cowboy team. "That's the sorriest pro football team ever assembled and it's coached by the sorriest coaching staff you could put together.

"Hold on there Cowboy, said Professor. If you were the owners of the Cowboys - what would you do to improve them?"

Well coach, I'm glad you asked that cause I've given it a lot of thought and this is what I've come up with.

First - I would run the team as a <u>business</u> and follow sound business principals. Therefore, the first step would be to find and hire a good business manager (some call him general manager).

Second - I would have a <u>team</u> only - no hotshots or super stars. My goal would be to keep fresh players in the game at all times and to be innovative and "different." The team would basically be a "Blue collar " team. If possible, I would have a second team - in the Arena Football League.

Finally - I would seek out and hire only <u>innovative</u> and "open minded" coaches and reward them well - probably pay them more than the players.

Now, let me expand upon these points. Before I begin however, I freely admit that I don't know all the NFL rules so I would try to find a good law firm that did and hire them before starting on the following projects:

1. Finding a good general manager - I would turn this over to professional head hunters and see what they came up with. If I didn't like the results, I would try to "lure" a good one from one of the more successful NFL clubs.

2. If possible to own both an NFL team and an arena league or foreign team I would do so and have a parent team - farm team set up. (much like baseball). This also depends on the rules about <u>moving</u> players. My

objective would be to <u>always</u> keep <u>healthy</u> and <u>fresh</u> players on the field.

Assuming that these things are possible, I would next establish a pay scale for each team and a bonus and profit sharing plan.

The pay scale would be based upon position played and would have automatic increases built in for years of experience. There would not be a large difference between positions. There would be large incentive team bonuses to be shared. And there would be a very rewarding profit sharing plan for all. Included in the bonus plan would be special cash rewards for such things as (a) obtaining college degrees (b) community service (c) team promotion. The concept is to build "Team First" thinking. If the team is successful - all win. If not - all don't.

The concept carries over to drafting and scouting. The scouts would be looking for <u>team</u> players - not superstars. The major attributes they would seek out would be (a) size (b) speed (c) strength (d) intelligence and (e) good morals. More than likely, any high draft choices would be traded. Also, most of the players you draft will be from "small" schools.

3. The key to success in this system would be coaching. The coaches would be well paid and they too would participate in the bonus program.

The basic schemes I would propose and the type of players to fit the schemes would be as follows:

<u>Defense</u>

4 Down linemen - I would look for <u>4</u> large "Blocks of stone" type that could win the line of scrimmage battle.

4 Line backers - I would look for <u>4</u> tall, fast, strong and aggressive players who could tackle an elephant and get to a quarterback before he could say "Aw crap".

2 Corner backs - Tall, speed burners, and smart.

1 Safeties - Fast and <u>smart</u> - their job would be to prevent <u>long</u> gains by the other team - period.

A safety would be in charge of the defense.

<u>Offense</u>

5 Down linemen - I would look for 5 giant - bulldozer types. (These are the <u>most</u> <u>important</u>

3 Receivers - Fast and good hands - size not that important.

1 Quarterback - Smart and good arm.

2 Backs - Good runners, good blockers, and pass catchers.

The offensive success would depend more on the game plan and play selection rather than individual players. I would always expect to <u>surprise</u> the opponent. Further, I would always be very aggressive with play selection.

For example, I would study the complete <u>history</u> of football and pull out some old plays, etc. from the past and practice them. i.e. The "Single Wing" (Neyland - Tennessee), "Quick Kicks", T-formation, statue of Liberty, etc. Ideally, the opponent would never know what to expect in <u>any</u> situation. I would never let the opponent's defense dictate my game strategy.

One of the assistant coaches would have a cell phone and all the game show "experts" as well as a few "experts" among the fans would have the phone number so they could call in during the game and "help" the coach. "That's a great idea" chuckled Ace.

On practically every third and long play - it would be "Bombs away". The quarterback would drop back and throw as far as he could toward either the right or left goal post (or other designated target). All the ends would try to get there and catch it. If it was intercepted, it would probably be further down field than a punt anyway.

And incidentally, all the ends would be instructed to do a hook on every play and the quarterback would be required to throw the ball on every passing play. (For example, if the play was a pass to the receiver or the left, and the pre-determined hook was "right" - if the quarterback thinks his receiver is covered when he is ready to throw - he throws to the right of the receiver.

The name of the game is to win and to entertain!! I think folks are tired of a loser and the same old "game plans" - for 16 weeks each year.

Geek asked "Why are the Cowboys so important anyway - I don't care that much about them?" "They say - its only a game."

Abe responded "It is far more than a game. Throughout the world folks have a <u>team</u> they follow and support. Their mood and attitude is greatly affected by the team's success or failure. Notice after a Cowboy game - if they win, everyone is happy and in a good mood. If they lose, everyone is unhappy and in a foul mood. That's just people." And I'll tell you for certain - unless you put some serious dollar pressure on J. Jones - he ain't about to change.

Ace said "that could happen if the Mavericks win another championship on two and the Rangers win a couple of World Series. "Don't forget the Stars" added Professor.

CHAPTER 8

ARE YOU READY FOR SOME (MORE) FOOTBALL?

It was raining the day of the September meeting and the temperature had fallen down to the mid 80's after staying over the 100 mark for nearly a month. As the crowd began to file in the meeting room. Everyone was happy and friendly.

"Did you watch the Saints games last night?" Inquired Ace – "They looked good." "They looked O.K. But they ain't got a chance – Tampa Bay still has a power house" answered Cowboy. "Yeah, but they looked good compared to the Cowboy's " retorted Tony. "Heck, miss Phoebe's Sunday school flag team looks good compared to the Cowboy's" spoke up Cowboy.

You all won't be making fun of the Cowboy's much longer – the Big Tuna is going to build them back up into a power house in a couple more years." "Horse crap" said Cowboy, The Big Tuna as you call him won't last 2 years - it's just a matter of time before he clashes with Jerry "The football joke" Jones – and then leaves.

Abe said – "Changing the subject – Does everyone agree that television is the sorriest in the months that football, especially pro football, is not or T.V.?" "Ain't no doubt about that – especially for men folk viewers like us" crowded in Cowboy among all the positive responses to Abe's question.

My next question is this "is there any program on T.V. that you would watch if it ran opposite a pro football game?" There was silence while the crowd mulled over this thought provoking question. Finally, Ace cleared his throat and said "I might switch to a good old John Wayne movie if the football game was sorta dull." "Me too" echoed Tony. No one else spoke up.

"Here is what I'm getting at, "said Abe. "I believe the time is ripe to create another football league – like ole lamar Hunt did back in 1992 when he started the American football league. But the one <u>major</u> difference in the new league is that it would be created, managed, and controlled like a T.V. show - cause that's what it would be – a TV show!

Ok, I haven't worked out all of the details but I'll tell you what I've come up with so far. Let me have a piece of chalk so I can sort of outline my plan and not repeat myself. Ace handed him a piece of chalk and he wrote on the blackboard.

TV FL
(Television Football League)

- League Office – Absolute controller
- Franchises
- The Games
- Playing rules
- Player contracts
- The draft

League Office

The league office would maintain <u>absolute</u> control over the league. The commissioner would have dictatorial powers. The staff would be kept at a bare minimum as would overhead. The prevailing rule of the league would be protection and care of the players and a fair return on investment to all franchise owners. The T.V. contracts would be negotiated by the commissioner. Life, health and loss of revenue insurance plus a retirement plan would be maintained by the league (and billed to the franchises). Salary caps would also be set by the commissioner – there would be no "Super star" contracts.

Franchises

Initially, sixteen franchise would be sold in mid market cities that do not presently have NFL teams. (i.e. San Antonio, El Paso, Shreveport, Jackson, Birmingham, Marietta, Louisville, Knoxville, etc. – get the picture? Ticket prices would be set by the league office – all games would be played on natural turf! (For player safety and "Real" football atmosphere and look).

The Game

The league would be broken into two division – east and west. All games would be scheduled on week day nights (no conflicts with NFL or area college games).

The games would be scheduled for 2 hour duration – 4 quarters of 24 minutes for time outs (including T.V. time outs). Filler material would be available if the games ended sooner – the idea is to allow exact T.V. programming of 2 hours period. There would be no halftime. Coaches would be forced to make sideline adjustments.

<u>Playing Rules</u>
The major changes in the rules would be in scoring. The initial proposed changes in scoring are:

Event	Points
Touchdowns:	
From inside the 5	7
From inside the 20	8
From outside the 20	9
Extra points:	
Kicked	1
Run in	2
Pass	2
Field goals:	
Inside the 20	1
Inside the 30	2
Inside the 40	3
Inside the 50	4
Outside the 50	5
First downs	1
Turnover recovery	2
Blocked kick	2
Forced punt (points to defense)	1

touchdown scored by
   runback of punt or kick
   off   10

The idea is to create more scoring – thus more excitement and cut down on tied scores. In case of a tie at end of game – it would remain a tie.

The playoffs would be a round Robin (double elimination) among the top 4 teams (of which at least I must be from each division).

There would be no instant replay. However, coaches could later challenge calls (from game film) they believe decided the game outcome and the commissioner could overturn the score and outcome if a major screw up was made.

Player Contracts

Player contracts would be standardized and salary ranges would be set by the league. For example:

Quarterback   - $250,000 to $350,000
Running back - $200,000 to $300,000
Linemen   - $120,000 to $240,000
Kickers   - $100,000 to $200,000

There would be a salary cap of $10,000,000 per franchise. There would be a playoff bonus in the contract which would allocate the team's playoff proceeds 50% to the players and 50% to the owners.

There would be a protective provision in the contract to the effect if a player dishonors his contracts and jumped to the NFL he agrees to reimburse the franchise 10%   of his NFL contract(s) for 5 years.

The objective would be to put about 900 football players who were not grabbed by the NFL to work and maintain a competitive level of good, entertaining football.

There would also be standard contracts and salary ranges and caps for the coaching staff.

Player Draft

The rules for the draft would be about the same as the NFL rules – i.e. – worst record gets first pick, etc. However, should a team draft a player who would not sign a contract – they could swap him to another team for a comparable player.

"You know Abe, I think you might have a good idea there. Heck, it might even work. But you know they already got arena league football which is similar to what you come up with and it ain't exactly setting the world on fire." Said Pinch.

"Naw, it ain't the same. They play it inside in little ole piss ant basketball courts" retorted Abe. "What I got in mind is old fashioned smash mouth, pig skin, gang talklin, football played out in the open on <u>grass</u> - like it is supposed to be. The ticket prices would be kept low enough so folks would go to the games and the scoring system would make it more exciting to watch -especially on T.V. And like I said, it would be run like a T.V. show - cause that's what it would be."

"Well, if you was the pro-football God - what rule changes would you make?" asked Cowboy.

"To begin with, I would recognize it for what it is - and that's entertainment." And from that perspective, each game should be like a movie - that is - the ending should not be <u>predictable</u>. Winning should be based on who planned the best and tried the hardest on that given day.

Every team should have a <u>chance to win</u>." Notice, I didn't say every team should be <u>equal</u> - that's not possible. Folks love to root for an underdog and they love a come from behind victory - particularly if it includes last second heroics and miracles." You look like you are in deep thought Ace, what are you thinking?" Ace began.

I don't profess to be an expert on pro football. Matter of fact, I don't even know the rules (in any detail) that govern the teams. However, if I was a team owner I would try to convince the others to hire a "Brain Trust" to come up with suggestions to improve the game (entertainment). Some of the things I would propose they consider are:

1. Adding a sport "Fan" to the competition committee.
2. Increasing the <u>number</u> of players each team is allowed carry on its roster.

3. Carefully study the Canadian rules and consider adopting some of them. i.e.

Let an end get a running start before the ball is snapped.

4. Intentional personal injury - make the player causing the injury sit out until the injured player   r

Let me tell you what my basic concepts are:

1. I think it is a <u>team</u> sport and every member is equally important.

2. I think the game is more mental than physical.

3. I think a large part of player compensation should be based on <u>team</u> accomplishments (i.e. win/loss   c

Now, let's look at some specifics which fall under those concepts.

1. Team sport

I don't believe in super stars nor do I believe in paying exorbitant salaries to the so called "Super stars." The <u>negatives</u> (of having a super star) far outweigh the positives I think. First, under the salary cap, it's like putting all your eggs in one basket. You use too much of your allotted money on one player and can't afford many other really good players.   Second, there is a very negative psychological effect on the other members of the team.   And finally, when he gets hurt (and they all do) you are crap out of luck.

I would much prefer a team of 11 good athletes who are extremely well coached and motivated on the field than have 1 super star and 10 average not too well coached athletes on the field.

I would set a salary cap for each position as well as the requirements a player must have to receive it - and stick to it.

I would set up a fat profit sharing plan and make sure everyone understood it.

Finally, I would set up an "Incentive bonus program" based on team performance.

Finally, I would establish a "player evaluation" committee comprised of <u>elected</u> players. This committee would be empowered to <u>fire</u> any player at any time. It could also recommend the firing of any coach.

2. The mental part

Because I think the mental part of the game is so important I would test the prospective athletes for their mental capacity and ability before I put them under contract - or drafted them. Of course, I would continue to test their physical skills also.

But where I would really pay attention to mental abilities is selecting the coach and coaching staff. I would pay coaches way above the league averages and try to get the <u>smartest</u> staff assembled in the league.

Innovation would be the key word for the coaches. For example - I would expect the coaches for the offense to look into some of the following:

1. A 300 pound back for inside the 3 (like the fridge at Chicago a few years back).
2. The single wing formation (like Neyland used at Tennessee).
3. The "Quick Kick" for third downs inside your own 30.
4. "Designed "Hail Mary" pass plays.
5. Designed "Catch and Lateral" plays
6. More running back passes
7. Repeating plays during the game.

In other words, keep the opponent guessing (big time) and the fans excited.

On defense - the word would be "Attack and disrupt." We would concentrate on <u>creating</u> turn-overs - i.e. - fumbles and interceptions. Defensive players would be encouraged to take big risks and make big plays and would not be criticized if it didn't work.

And finally, the coaches would be instructed to never let up and try to sit on the lead. Much substitution would be encouraged - keep as much <u>fresh</u> talent on the field as possible.

I'm not sure this could be done within the rules or not - but I would look into it.

1. Buy an "Arena" football team.

2. When a player got hurt - "Loan" him to the arena team and "borrow" one of the arena players to take h

Pinch said, "You almost parroted Abe. Might work - might not; sounds exciting and entertaining anyway." Let's play some domino's - "Hut! Hut!"

CHAPTER 9

NINE - ONE - ONE
911
September 11th

At the last meeting in September, 2001, everyone arrived excited and full of talk about the terrible tragedies that had occurred on the 11th in New York and Washington.

"That's the damndest thing I ever heard of , expressed Ace, we ought to send our bombers over there and blow them camel jockeys to Hell."

"Yep, that's an attack on our country and that means war in my book" sided Cowboy.

"I saw the widow Barns at the grocery store in Bowie last Saturday and we were talking about it - she broke down and cried. One of her nephews worked in the

Pentagon and was killed when that plane crashed into it."

She is such a devout Christian lady that she was willing

to forgive the people responsible

- whoever they were." added Pinch.

"That's the problem we have here" said the old sage

Abe, "Whoever they are?" This is not a case of one

nation attacking another such as the Jap's attack on Pearl

Harbor, the Iraq's attack on Dubai, the Chinese attack on

Vietnam, etc. When you look back in history, wars were

started by nations (except for the Crusades maybe). No

nation has admitted responsibility or taken credit for the

9-11 disaster - and I don't believe they will. Our

intelligence has pointed the blame at the Al Quida and its

financial backer, Omar Bin Laden. We <u>must</u> get the facts

before we do something stupid.

CHAPTER 10

AW SHUCKS - I SHOULDN'T HAVE DONE THAT

Gullible George (Bush) sicked the dogs on the Iraquas yesterday, announced Professor, what do you think he is thinking today?

He's probably feeling purty proud of himself today, but I guarantee that a year from now he'll be thinking "Aw shucks I shouldn't a done that" spoke up Abe.

I don't know what he's thinking but I'll tell you what I'm thinking spoke up Professor "That was one of the stupidest mistakes I ever heard of - it was one of the darkest days in this country's history." "Amen" was the general response of the crowd.

Yep, George and his advisers, Rove, Cheney, etc. and the big oil company boys are swapping some of our soldier boys lives for oil. They might whip Saddam and his army but that ain't going to end the "war". Them folks will pick off our soldiers, one at a time, as long as they are over there occupying their land. Think about it - if the Iraq army had done the same thing to us Texans - don't you think we would make em pay for it. Heck yes - we would.

In a way, that might of been a good thing. Maybe the democrats can use it to wake us up and defeat Bush and the elephants in the next election?

"The heck of it is, us poor dumb taxpayers and our soldier boys pay the price for the politicians screw ups. The cost of the Iraq war is estimated to be 500 billion on some such inconceivable amount. And the army is going to be kept over there forever - or as long as they can pump oil out of the ground." Concluded Pinch.

"Yeah, and Bush can get down on his knees and beg the United Nations, to help out and they are going to say "Screw you Georgie boy" injected Abe.

"Aw heck, Bush will find some sucker third world country or countries that will send over their troops - for a price" said Professor.

"But as long as there are invaders there the Iraq are going to keep picking them off - one at a time" said Abe.

"Here are the questions I'd like answered "Said Cowboy.

*Who is getting the oil that is being pumped in Iraq?
*Who is getting the money from the sale of the Iraqi oil (assuming it is being sold of course)?

CHAPTER 11

WHAT CAUSES WARS?

"I wonder why folks is always fighting" inquired Cowboy "Dollars or economics" quickly responded Abe. Those that start wars are trying to take something away from them they are jumping on.

"That ain't always true" said Professor. What about when the Indians were always raiding and warring against the early settlers - right here in this country. All they took were scalps - and hair pierces weren't worth nothing.

"Professor, you are really showing your ignorance with that statement. Think about it. Who started the war? It wasn't the Indians. The settlers started the war when they forced the Indians off the land - they were fighting over possession of the land.   That fight goes back to the beginning of mankind.

Regardless of how or who created this planet we call Earth; deeds to the land were not handed out initially. Land was held by the strongest at the time. (and still is generally speaking). This concept of land ownership and formal process of recording title to the land is purely man made.

"Well, if you are so smart - tell me how we got to the point that you own this property we are standing on right now," interrupted Professor.

"You will have to use your imagination (which I realize is very limited) and I'll try to recreate the history of "ownership" of this property." said Abe.

Many thousands of years ago a caveman (who we will call Brutus wandered through here and stopped by Clear

Creek which runs through the south side of this property. He found that shallow cave on the bluff by the creek and killed a snake with a rock and ate it. Then he found some berries which he ate. Next, he raked some leaves in the cave and made a bed and said to himself "This is my new home." He roamed around the area for days and days - hunting for something to eat. But every night he returned to the cave to sleep. One morning when he got up, there was another cave man standing outside the cave - looking in. Old Brutus grabbed a stick and jumped up and ran toward the newcomer yelling #;;;#!! (Cave man talk for "Get the heck outta here - this is my property). He managed to whack the interloper across the head one good lick before he got away.

A few other cavemen wandered thru the next few years but Brutus and his stick successfully chased them off.

Then one day a cave woman showed up and crawled into his bed of leaves just before dark. When Brutus crawled into the cave it was already dark. He smelled her before he felt her. She was in heat and nature took over. She didn't run so Brutus slid into bed with her and seduced her. Before he knew what was happening - he was married to her and she followed him everywhere he went after that. In nine months she dominoed and produced Brutus Junior.

Brutus taught Brutus, Jr. how to hunt and fish and use a stick for a club. He taught him how to yell at intruders and whack them on the head with the stick to run them off and to protect their property.

This was repeated for several generations while the cave men owned this ranch.

Then one day, a couple of advanced cavemen (early Indians) showed up. One of them carried a sharpened longer stick (spear) and the other carried a small stick with a big rock attached to the end of it (Tomahawk). When the caveman ran at them shouting #;!#; they didn't run. They shouted back ; - #

and one of them rammed his spear into the caveman's gut and the other bashed his brains out with his tomahawk. That's how the Indians bought this property. They held on to it for a few hundred years until a whole tribe showed up, equipped with bows and arrows, and bought it from the bunch that was still using sharpened sticks and clubs.

They held on to the property for the next few hundred years until it was claimed by Mexico. Nobody from Mexico actually moved on to the property - the Indians still lived here. Then the Spaniards, who called themselves conquistadors, whipped up on the Mexicans and claimed the property for a while - till the Mexicans whipped back upon them. During all this time of whipping - the Indians lived here. However, the Spaniards had brought some horses with them and some of them got loose. Another bunch of Indians, the Comanche's, caught some of them wild horses and learned how to ride them. One day a bunch of them showed up on horseback and chased all the ones afoot off and claimed all this country as their own. But before long the toughest of the lot showed up - the Texans.

The Texans, who had guns and horses, whipped up on the Mexicans and jumped on the Indians. They fought back and forth until the Texans joined up with the United States. (The Government).

The Government sent its horse soldiers (cavalry) down to protect the Texans and they did this by whipping up on the Indians. By then they had rapid shouting firearms, including Gatling guns, and the pore ole Indians didn't have a prayer.

The Government took over this land and set up a system of land title recording and gave a big chunk of it to the railroad to get them to build a railroad through here. Course the railroad didn't need but a small strip of the land to lay the truck on so the carved off the rest of it and sold off chunks of it. This ranch was a part of a big chunk that was purchased by a group of fellers from Scotland who ran cattle on it for about twenty years - tile the plague durn near broke them. They lost all their cows and divided the land up into smaller parcels and sold them off. By then, Texas was a state and had been divided up into counties. Title to the land was recorded in records kept at the county court house.

You can go to the courthouse in Jacksboro and look it up. You will see that the Scotchmen sold this particularly parcel of land to Leon Shelby in October, 1848. Shelby later sold the property to Boaz Hamilton in March, 1878. The property stayed in the lands of the Hamilton Family (passed on from one generation to the next) until Lester Box bought it from Boaz Hamilton's grandchildren in April 1995.

And that, Mr. Carpenter, is the history of this piece of property. There is a story very similar to this connected to almost ever chunk of land on this Earth. Just about every speck of dirt has been the cause of a war or wars.

More recent wars were fought over resources which were an internal part of the land.

So how do you stir up an entire nation to jump on another nation? Simple --just convince them the grass is greener over yonder - and we deserve it - we were destined to own it. Then declare war.

Heck, the "Americans" didn't have any trouble convincing themselves it was ok to kill off the dirty Redskins and taking title to the land. It was their "manifest destiny." God said it was O.K., hadn't the Indians taken it away from old Brutus.

I guess the moral of the story is - "If you want something bad enough and if it is worth enough money - you can always find some way to justify it and to get Gods stamp of approval on it." Concluded Professor.

CHAPTER 12

THE NATION'S (AND WORLD'S) PRIORITIES

"How long do you think the United States can maintain its position as the dominant world power?" Is the world going to come to an end?" If so, when and how? This was the challenge of the day that Tony hurled at the group to wake them up on hot August day. Although most were on their 3rd or 4th cup of coffee they all looked sleepy and lifeless.

"What should we, as a nation, be doing right now?

Cowboy was the first to take the bait and he spoke up strongly saying "Heck fire - I think the good ole U.S.A. will always be the best and strongest country and I don't think the world will end - ever!"

"We got a quick response from Cowboy. Anyone else agree with him" asked Abe.

"Heck no" responded Tony. Professor didn't stop to think much before he spoke up - "Else he doesn't know much history or is just plain stupid."

"What does history have to do with it" demanded Cowboy.

"Everything" responded Professor. "If you go back through recorded history you can clearly see that nations grow to the positions of world powers but without exception - each of them fell off the throne for one reason or another. "Some were defeated and replaced by a new empire and some were destroyed from within. From memory I'll tell you about many of them (starting with the most recent) and the brief history of each."

1997 - British Empire - The handover ceremony (Hong Kong to China) is generally considered to be the end of the empire. At its height in 1922, the British Empire included about 1/4 of the world's population and land area. There were actually two British Empires - 1583 to 1783 and 1783 to 1815. The Empire was held together by the largest and best navy in the world. The end of the Empire was caused by many wars and many of its possessions gaining independence over a long period of time. The rise of the U.S. A. had a lot to do with the fall of British powers and controls.

1991 - USSR - Communism collapses in the Soviet Union and it breaks up into states. Several of these states later joined the Europe Union. The collapse was basically bankruptcy caused by the "Cold War" with the U.S.A.

1947 - Empire of Japan - The Japanese Empire was built by conquest starting in 1868. At its height, it ruled over 2,857,000 square miles of land area that included Taiwan, Korea, Manchuria and parts of Northern China. The Empire ended when Japan surrendered to the allies in 1947.

1945 & 1918 - Empires of Germany - There were two German Empires. The first, under Kaiser Wilhelm II was from 1868 to1918 and the second was under Adolph Hitler and the Nazis from 1933 to 1945. Hitler took control of much of Europe diplomatically simply by threatening war - and much by military conquest. (Czechoslovakia, Poland, Bohemia, Moravia, and Lithuania). The Empire came to an end in 1945 when Germany surrendered to the allies.

1922 - Ottoman Empire - The Ottoman Empire was one of the largest and longest lasting (1299 to 1922) in history. It was an Empire inspired and sustained by Islam and Islamic institutions with its capital in Constantinople. Its end came with the Turkish war of independence.

1819 - Spanish Empire - The Spanish Empire began in appx 1520 and ended in April 1819. The empire was built by parts of exploration, conquest, and colonization and included Mexico, parts of the now U.S.A., Cuba, most of South America and Central America. It ended in defeat in the Spanish - American war.

1815 - French Empire - The French Empire began in 1804 when Napoleon was the emperor. France was the dominant power of most of Europe during the early 19th Century. At its peak it controlled most of Germany,

Spain, Italy, Poland, and Australia. It's demise began who it invaded Russia and ended with Napoleon's defeat at the Battle of the Waterloo (by England).

1227 - Mongol Empire (Genghis Khan) - Khan created an empire from the Nomadic tribes of Northeast Asia which spread eastward up to present day Europe.

5th Century - Roman Empire - There has been more written on the rise and fall of the Roman Empire than practically any other subject. However, the reasons, etc. are basically theory. The most common "Guess" is simply moral decay. One of the most famous writers, Coward Gibbon, placed the blame on the loss of civic virtue among the roman citizens who entrusted the role of defending the empire to barbarian mercenaries who eventually turned on them.

And there were others of less magnitude or importance.

"The United States is now on the top of the mountain but it is a safe bet to say it will topple someday. And then another nation will rise up to take the world throne" concluded Professor.

"What nation do you think that will be:" asked Tony.

"The best guess would be China but other candidates would be A re-united Russia, A United South America, A United Africa, Canada, Australia, India, United Religious Order (i.e. Islam's) or who knows" answered Professor.

"Why can't the USA stay in control - it is so strong that I just can't conceive it even toppling" commented Pinch.

"It probably won't topple, responded Professor, "It will probably implode" I don't think another nation will destroy the USA - I think it will "Suicide itself" (as old

Dick Long use to describe it)". We are already in a period of devolution and going downhill fast.

That may be true, agreed Ace, but before that happens, what should we, as a nation try to accomplish? what should be our national priorities?"

Some of the things I have always believed our country should have concentrated on, which I will name later, would help all of mankind now and forever in the future. If they could be accomplished they would also add to world peace I believe.

These projects are -

(1) Figure out a way to harness the energy of the sun. This is the <u>ultimate</u> energy source - can't everybody see that!

(2) Convert the salt water in to the oceans to fresh water and pipe it inland to arid regions (use the sun's energy for the power to drive the pumps).

(3) Expand medical research to cure <u>all</u> diseases and improve health. Encouraged the use of <u>natural</u> stuff and technical/mechanical and don't depend entirely on chemistry and drugs.

(4) Clean up our government and our laws.

(5) Stay the heck out of other countries affairs - don't be so "know it all" - learn to mind our own business. I'm a firm believer in my grandpa's opinion - "Be the biggest and toughest dog in the bunch and you will <u>never</u> have any trouble with any of the other dogs - never." In modern terms, that means if we maintain military superiority no other country is going to bother us - leave them alone and they will leave us alone.

"That all I got to say on the subject" said Professor.

"There's some darn good ideas" expressed Abe, "I'd say if we could get them accomplished, history would be good to us - especially if we could solve all the other problems we've talked about."

"Time for dominos" said Cowboy.

CHAPTER 13

WHAT THIS COUNTRY REALLY NEEDS IS A ....

The December domino session had all the early signs of doom and disaster. It was three days until Christmas and a blizzard had passed through the night before and dumped about 8 inches of snow on the north Texas country side. Furthermore, the blue northern which pushed the blizzard through had brought an ample supply of extremely cold air and the temperature was hovering near 0." The snow was a welcomed sight because the countryside had been under a severe drought for over a year and all the grass was long gone. Hay had sky rocketed to $100 a roll (big round bale) and most everyone had sold most of their livestock.

Even though Abe had arrived early and had a roaring fire going in the pot bellied stove, a big pot of hot coffee brewed, and the domino parlor was warm and cozy - everyone that entered was in a grumpy mood.

Anybody watch the cowboy game Sunday? Inquired Cowboy. "Yep", replied Pinch, - except it wasn't no game - it was a joke - them overpaid prima donnas couldn't beat Miss Phoebe's ballet class in a game of football." "I agree, said Tony, this is three years running that they won 5 and lost 11 - so long as Jones runs the show they are going to stay the laughing stock of the NFL. "I told you all what it was going to take to win (see Chapter 8) "spoke up Cowboy."

"Aw heck, I don't want to hear anymore about that sorry fake football team" said Tony, "Let's talk about something else today." "What do you suggest?" Asked Abe. Well, I'd like to hear some ideas on what the government should be doing about the future - how they should be spending our money - and so forth."

I remember (just barely) a professor in college talking about the human race eventually screwing itself out of existence. He based his sermon on the views of an ancient economist named Malthus - or something like that. I think he called it the Malthusian theory that said - people would keep screwing, and keep screwing and reproducing to the point that the food supply wouldn't support them and they would all starve. With the drought we've had around here and the drastic decrease in beef production - I can see where that could happen - real easy. All of this rambling was laid it on the boys by Cowboy.

"Aw horse apples," boomed in Professor. There's gazillions of acres of this old earth that could produce food that ain't even been touched. Your problem, Cowboy, is that you think Texas is the whole Earth - and it ain't - not by a long shot.

"That's all you know smart Alec - grumbled Cowboy. I was in the service and went overseas. But heck fire, all you got to do is drive out to west Texas and you will see jillions of acres of raw land that ain't producing nothing."

"Well dummy, that(cough) because (cough) there ain't no water out there" - coughed in Tony. Darn, I wish I could get rid of this darn cough he added. I was in Dallas the other day and saw a bunch of them cardboard box dwellers (homeless) under a bridge and it looked like they was having a coughing contest."

Changing the subject slightly - I stopped at Shorty's Conoco Station this morning and put gas in my tank - that stuff has gone up 40¢ a gallon since I put some in last week. I raised cain with Shorty about it and he said it was costing him 40¢ more a gallon and he was only passing his cost on to us consumers - and that he wasn't making a red cent off the increase. He claims the distributor told him the price had gone up because of "war fears;" can you believe that crap? If the drought don't break us - the price of gasoline will."

It seems to me that you boys have come up with a whole list of problems that the government could be working on instead of trying to create another war. These problems all center on the basic needs of mankind for survival (a) food (b) shelter (c) water (d) energy and (e) clothing. The only thing you left out was sex but I guess that isn't a problem.

"Back on the main track" interrupted Professor. There are plenty of resources to solve all of the above mentioned problems if we could just figure out how to use them. If my memory serves me, the surface of the Earth is made up of 75% water and 25% land and about 1/3 of the land isn't being used. Furthermore, we wake up to the ultimate source of energy each morning - the sun!

Now it seems to me that what the government ought to be doing is:

(1) Figuring out an economical way of capturing and using the sun's energy.

(2) Figuring out a way to desalinate the water in the oceans.

(3) Figuring out a way to transport the desalinated water from the shorelines to the arid interior regions where it is most needed. and

(4) Figuring out how to build inexpensive shelters from the most plentiful ingredient available - and that is dirt.

"You left out one thing Professor, "said Tony." And what is that? haughtily responded Professor. "How to cure a cold" said Tony.

Just think, continued Tony. If the government just set aside 1 year and said "we are going to take all the money we have been wasting for war stuff, foreign aid, and other useless crap "and if industry said "we are going to spend our research dollars trying to solve the above mentioned problems instead of creating a newer and faster method of communications, different looking SUV's, etc." they could probably get the job done.

I happen to know, Professor, that folks have been working on those things for a long time and have had some success. Heck, I can go to Tractor Supply and buy "Solar panels" that use the sun to supply electricity for an electric fence. And my wife showed me an article in a National Geographic a while back that showed where some of them rich Arabs had created fresh water from ocean saltwater and had irrigated there desert so much it looked like a tropical rain forest.

"I am quite aware of those things" said Professor. However, the missing ingredient so far has been "Economic feasibility." That is why additional research is necessary. Edison created a device that produced light using electricity long before "Light bulbs" were used in the home. He had to do much research before he stumbled upon tungsten as the magic ingredient for the bulbs. Maybe there is a better way to capture and use the sun's energy than the solar panel/or other technique's they are trying to perfect. And maybe there is a better way to get salt out of ocean water than the evaporation process. And maybe there is a better way to use dirt as a building material.

But think for a minute what it would be like if we had a large solar powered desalination facility down around Corpus Christy that created fresh water from the gulf of Mexico and pumped it through a gigantic pipeline (again using solar energy to provide power for the pumps) out to say Pecos and there used it for irrigation of millions of acres of farmland. Heck, they could about feed the world. "Aye Gawd, I think you've got something there Professor "spoke up Pinch.

But what about my cold? Asked Tony. Well, it's obvious that the chemist aren't going to solve the problem said Ace. They have come up with more cold medicines, antibiotics, anti histamines, etc. etc. than you can shake a stick at and the common cold is still around and the chemical companies are getting richer. Maybe it's time we put the rocket scientist on this project. Suppose, for example, they created a machine that you could walk up to, put on a face mask and breathe into it for a couple minutes, and walk away "cured" from your cold. The machine would clean the air you expelled and kill all the germs using beta rays or some such. Why hasn't this been done? Money! Think of the billions of dollars it would cost the drug companies if there were no longer "common colds."

Remember what I said about all decisions being based on dollars (See Chapter 4). Said Pinch.

Let's play domino's! said Cowboy.

Maybe it would be better to have the desalination plant out in the desert and pump the salt water to it," said Tony rather weakly.

Abe said "I'm 72 years old and I've lived through a terrible depression and several wars but I don't think I've ever seen this country as screwed up as it is today. It seems like every time the Republicans are in control in Washington, the economy just turns to crap". Anybody want to comment?"

Professor said "I do - I've always voted Republican because I'm a conservative and I've lived almost as long as you - I remember how Roosevelt sent folks out in this country and had folks kill livestock and plow under crops and things were mighty bad - so don't blame the Republicans for the mess we are in - blame Roosevelt and the liberal Democrats.

"Professor, that is the most illogical statement I've heard since Bush gave his reasons for attacking Iraq.

Abe interrupted, with his usual profound logic "That's a big part of the problem - finger pointing and trying to place blame. In the final analysis - the voters themselves must accept the blame because they were gullible enough to elect the idiot who screwed things up. What this country needs is direction and strong leadership - and the voting masses to recognize both."

"Well professor, if you are so darn smart, tell us what direction you would point us in if it was up to you" spoke up Cowboy.

The Professor stated - "It would be nice to turn back the clock and go back to the old isolationist policy (speak low and wield a big stick) to keep the rest of the world in check. But that is not the answer. The world has shrunk so and technology has advanced so that we must now deal with the <u>global</u> economy instead of only the U.S. economy. The key then becomes "trying to pull the rest of the world up to our standards of living instead of letting them pull us down to their standards in the process. But I think it must be done if we are to remain a world power. Incidentally, I believe we have already begun the decline (as a world power) - but that's another subject for debate.

First, let me go over a few things I would do in dealing with the rest of the world. Next I'll deal with internal matters.

<u>Dealing with the rest of the world</u>:

1. Trade - but don't give anything away. In the past the U.S.A. has literally given away trillions of dollars believing we were gaining a friend and ally for our money. Didn't work. We need to be trading goods <u>and</u> services to them in exchange for raw materials or labor.

2. Turn loose <u>advertising</u> on the world - create a demand for <u>our</u> products and services.
(If we can't get back into the manufacturing business we are doomed).

3. <u>Force</u> increased standards on other countries - i.e. civil rights, fringe benefits, minimum wages, etc.

<u>Internal (USA) matters</u>:

1. Raise taxes - drastic increase for wealthy who hoard money but create tax relief if they invest it and create jobs.

2. Create a national health care program that makes sense and works.

3. Rebuild the railroads - dual lines (freight and passenger)

4. Tax the heck out of autos and trucks

5. Develop mass transit systems

6. Rebuild our manufacturing capacity.

7. Re -regulate certain industries:
   *Utilities
   *Air travel
   *Communications

8. <u>Feed the world</u> - improve U.S. agriculture.

9. Learn to build affordable shelter for the poor.

10. Get back to God.

Pinch said "That all sounds good but here is one dilemma you did not address or answer.

If we don't get our Federal Government straightened out and run more like a business - we are absolutely going bankrupt."

Pinch responded "That's not going to happen - that was Ross Perot's message if you remember - and very few paid any attention to him. Another problem we haven't discussed is lobbyist. We need to somehow brand them, make them report and be accountable for their deeds, and tax the heck out of them.

Oh yeah, I forget to mention - all politician's and judges should be limited to three terms in office - none of which can be consecutive.

CHAPTER 14

OUR GOVERNMENT "SUCKS"

"Wal, said Pinch, "what do you fellers think of the Bush administration now - especially you who voted them in?" This question created an uproar on this hot August morning. Everyone started babbling at once.

Finally, Cowboy, in his booming voice, quitted the crowd with his conclusion - <u>Our</u> <u>government</u> <u>sucks</u> it don't make no difference <u>who</u> we send to Washington - the result is always the same. Big business with all its power (i.e. money) really runs the show and they finally get to the majority of the Washington crowd and have them dancing like puppets to whatever tune they decide to play. And you can bet the tune will line their pockets at the expense of the "average" citizen - who the heck that might be.

"Yeah, but it's still a lot better living in this country than say Cuba - where ole Castro runs everything" defended Tony.

"How do you know? "Quizzed Professor - "You ain't even been to Cuba.

"That's a true fact admitted Tony, but I saw a show on TV a couple of weeks ago about Cuba and them folks looked like they lived about like that wetback family that lives in a tent down on Crooked Creek."

"Do you believe everything you see on TV?" countered Professor. "Heck, all the media is controlled by big business and Jews, and politicians and they constantly brainwash the public. I've got so I watch more shows on cable that come from Mexico or Europe than I do the American shows – specially news. It sure gives you a different slant on things.

I think the problem is simply – this country has lost its morals. It seems like everything goes anymore – long as you got money to pay a good lawyer. Look at O.J. Simpson, the Enron bunch and soon Kobe Bryant. They kill, steal, and rape without any consequence."

"Would you rather have some Catholic priest in charge – or maybe a Queer Episcopal Bishop?" asked Ace.

"Heck no," retorted Professor – but that's my point. The moral decay has spread throughout our society."

"I'll tell you what, aye gawd, interrupted Pinch, I know that I was a heck of a lot better off under Slick Willie and the Democrats than I am under gullible George and the Republican. "So am I echoed" Cowboy, then Professor.

"That's because the government checks you got for not growing wheat were bigger then" countered Abe.

"Hold on boys," strongly commanded Pinch, "Let's save that argument for another day." We've got all we can handle today just talking about our government is general. Abe, you've been quiet all morning, we would like to hear your thoughts on the subject.

Abe spoke, "I can't think of a more complex subject this morning and I get a migraine headache just thinking about it. I'll probably confuse everyone here if I start rambling but you requested my thoughts and I'll try to unscramble them and get them somewhat organized in this old scarred cranium of mine before I commence. Please bear with me a few moments. (He got up – poured himself another cup of coffee, lit a cigarette, and scrabbled a few things on a pad before he looked up and addressed the room full of anxious listeners.

"First, history repeats itself. From the days of the earliest recorded history of this planet earth there have been powers rise up and dominate for a while and then fade to be followed by another power which goes through the same cycle followed by another, etc., etc, Remember professors discussion about past world powers a couple of months ago and how they dominated the world (Earth) for a time and analyzed the <u>source</u> of their power and the reason for their downfall.

I'm not going to repeat Professors history lesson of our world – I realize that he summarizing thousands of years of history and left out much of what happened over that time span. The point I want to make is "crap happens and things change." No world power has yet to remain such for an extremely long period of time – and probably none ever will. In my opinion, the United States "peaked" as a world power when Russia collapsed and it has been going downhill ever since. How long it takes for us to be replaced by another power (and my guess is that power will be oriental – probably Chinese) is anyone's guess – maybe another 100 years – maybe only 50 – maybe longer – who knows-maybe tomorrow – we certain aren't gaining any popularity throughout the world and if everyone in the world voted on it, it's certainly that <u>we</u> <u>would</u> <u>lose</u> if the vote were honestly and accurately tabulated. A lot more foreign folks hate us than admire us – and most with good reason.

Second, despite all the efforts to force "democracy" and it's principals and ideals upon the world; the fact remains that the law on the jungle dominates. It is still a struggle for survival and survival of the fittest. And we may not be the fittest!

Third, we haven't learned how to use and live with the technology that has been developed. Some of it is more damaging than valuable and much of it is wasted.

Fourth, the pursuit of profit and the worship of the almighty dollar is ruining us as a nation and as a people, that is the main reason our morals have gone to heck.

Finally, our citizens are fat, dumb, and happy and really don't give a darn about what goes on in Washington – or anywhere else in the world – unless it affects them directly!

Shucks Abe, you ain't told us much that we didn't already know. But so far, it don't explain why our government sucks as Cowboy put it.

That's true, but you have to remember that most of us here are old farts. We've all started our lives in a major depression, been through a <u>world</u> war plus several lesser wars, and seen enough technological changes to blow your mind. Not many folk see things they way we do and none of them think like we do; matter of fact, they think we're a bunch of idiots.

"Yep, I agree that everyone else is nuts except maybe you and me – and right now I'm starting to wonder about you." answered Pinch. Let me ask you a question "What one thing do you believe is responsible for the screwed up status of the world today?

Abe thought a minute and replied "The creation of the atomic bomb."

"Explain that please" asked Ace.

Well, there are several factors to consider. First, it meant that the most powerful nation no longer was the one with the most natural resources or the greatest population. Second, it placed a premium on science and technology.   And, it created a feeling of fear and insecurity in people's minds.   They realized how vulnerable they were to destruction (death) and started thinking - God can't save us from that thing; I'd better enjoy life to the fullest as quick as I can – enjoy today and don't worry about tomorrow.   And gather as much stuff as you can as soon as you can – legally or otherwise.

And the next bad thing that happened was plastic. Plastic gave us the ability to create credit cards and credit cards gave everyone the ability to collect a heck lot of stuff.

What it really comes down to is "State of mind." And the powers that be are only concerned with lining their pockets with as much money as they can – the public be

darned. And the public is trying to do the same thing –
the government be darned included.

Cowboy inquired "Can anyone explain to me how
economics works and how the government affects
economics?"

The Professor said "It is such a complicated thing and I
don't believe   there is anyone who completely
understands it. Well I see folks on TV all the time that
sound like experts to me injected Cowboy.

"That is because they are talking about one little sliver
of the economy which many honesty feel they understand
- however, they don't have a clue to the domino effect it
might have on other segments. answered Professor.

"You just went over my head" said Cowboy. "Let me
give you a couple of illustrations from things I heard on
TV just this week, responded Professor. A well know

inventor of the Iphone and other electronic gadgets died this week and the news commentator was giving him credit for creating millions of new jobs. Let's analyze that for a minute.

1. Were new jobs created - sure, mostly computer programmer jobs.

2. What jobs were destroyed?

(a) Many people shut off their land line phones and the land line companies had to cut back - technical and semi skilled people.

(b) Many people switched to selling and advertising on the Iphones, newspapers, magazines, ad agencies, the post office, etc. had to "cut back" because of the lost business."

This is happening every day - improvements in technology is literally destroying jobs. Also, the government was proposing to rebuild our interstate highway system - in order to create new jobs. While it is true this temporarily creates jobs - it likewise cost the taxpayers one heck of a lot in taxes.

CHAPTER 15

LIES AND SMOKE AND MIRRORS

After the usual shuffle, filling coffee cups, etc. Pinch asked Does anyone pay any attention to commercials and the news anymore?" The general consensus – not really. Pinch said – "That's good – I'm proud of you – cause all we are fed is a bunch of lies and half truths and misleading information".

"What the heck are you talking about?" Asked Cowboy.

Pinch replied "Don't you realize this nation declared and tried to justify war on a much, much, inferior nation based upon lies and deceit by our leaders?" And by the way, that is not the first time in our history that's been done. There's a good reason the rest of the world calls us "The ugly Americans." And there is a trickledown effect of this lying. Just pay attention to the next TV commercial you watch – there is a probability it is either a pure lie or deceitful".

I'm fearful we are in the late stages of moral decay and it may be <u>too</u> <u>late</u> to save us. Lies and deceit now seem to me to be the rule rather than the exception. Also, in my view, our own center of government (Washington DC) is the most sinful and downright criminal place on the face of the earth."

Ace spoke up, "that's purty powerful stuff Pinch – give us some examples and tell us what you believe got us to this position."

"Ok, replied Pinch, I'll use 2008 to give you some examples.

1. The price of oil and gas - Opec lied about capacity and concealed new supplies and the U.S. oil companies chimed right in. Oil shot up to almost $150 a barrel and gasoline to nearly $4 a gallon. When the truth became known oil dropped to under $40.
2. The car manufactures came out with a little high mileage hybrid car they said would pollute less and save fuel. Pollution wise, it is highly debatable when you consider how much energy is used to make the batteries and how much carbon dioxide is emitted. And some didn't get as many MPG as their fustic fossil fuel powered equivalents.
3. Deregulation was a big mistake - really a joke. (That's Reaganomics for you). His trickledown economics was a sham.
4. Comparing today's problems with the great depression is another political joke. There is no comparison.
5. And finally, if all the lies that Obama said about Hillary Clinton were true – why did he appoint her as secretary of state?

How and why did we become so deceitful and corrupt? Here is my theory-
There has always been a little good and a little evil in

all of us – going back to the cave man. I agree with Abe

that the one event in history that swung the pendulum to "evil" was the dropping of the atom bomb. People suddenly realized how <u>uncertain</u> life on this earth could be so they decided they should accumulate as much wealth as they could (regardless of the means) and enjoy life to the <u>fullest</u>.

Can I add my two cents worth? Asked Pinch. Everyone yelled "Hail yes Pinch – cut loose".

Pinch began "our nation is going through an era which the news media describes as the era of the baby boomers. In my opinion, a more apt title would be "era of lies, deceit, and hand outs" or "era of smoke and mirrors." Every one lies to you these days – particularly politicians and T.V. ads. The mind set of most of the so called baby boomers is about 180 degrees from ours (meaning us old farts)."

Geek got red in the face and said "Dad, how can you say that? You've got to explain yourself."

Pinch gave him a stern look and said "Sit down son and turn off that stupid I phone and listen for a change.

When I was a young man and a business man came to me for advice when his business was not turning a profit – we usually advised greater <u>sales</u> effort. Next was greater efficiency followed by cost reductions. Today it appears they go about it in exactly the reverse order – and I suspect that is also what is being taught in colleges. And even the approach is different. In the old days if a company had to lay off employees to reduce costs – they always laid off the ones with the least seniority. Today they start by laying off the highest paid. It is a brutally cold process and loyalty means <u>absolutely</u> <u>nothing</u>.

The new laws coming out of our congress have also taken a different slant – instead of <u>thou</u> <u>shalt</u> <u>not</u> laws most of them now a days are <u>thou</u> <u>shalt</u>. Good example – when you operate or ride in a vehicle <u>thou</u> <u>shalt</u> wear a seat belt. Where is this dictatorial approach taking us? How do we stop it?

All the young people would be lost without those darn Iphones. They are constantly texting, or talking on them. If they ever got out in the woods and the battery went dead on their Iphone – they couldn't find their way home. And in another generation or two – there won't be <u>any</u> thinkers left – just a bunch of robotic looking people with an I phone in their hand.

Now, I'll shut up and listen".

"Let's close up and go home" suggested Abe.

CHAPTER 16

SLOW LEARNERS

"Does anyone remember how George Bush stole the presidential election in 2000 from ole what's his name?" Is how Professor started the conversation at the mid August domino game.

"I remember something about the votes in Florida" responding Tony "But I forgot the details" "Yep, and his brother was governor in Florida at the time" added Cowboy.

"Don't you realize by now that politics is the nastiest and meanest business in the whole wide world?" asked Abe. "And Americans are probably the laziest and most uncaring bunch around. They have never experienced hardship, hunger, warfare up close, and all the bad stuff that other folks on the planet earth must endure. As a consequence; they are mighty slow learners "he added.

"Aw, I wouldn't say they are slow learners so much has they just don't give a darn" challenged Tony. He observed "What was it ole Lyndon (Johnson – 40th president) once said? All you got to promise them is a big platter of BBQ, comfortable pair of tennis shoes, and a warm place to take a crap and you got their vote."

"I think Lyndon was referring to a special segment of voters" injected Abe, "Nevertheless, the point is well made. So long as an American has his personal needs fulfilled (or is promised to have them fulfilled without any serious effort on his part) he is satisfied and not apt to get too excited about nothing. But threaten to take his stuff and he becomes the toughest and meanest critter there is".

"You fellers are getting off the subject" objected Pinch. Let's concentrate on voting for a few minutes." "What the heck is there to discuss about voting? asked Professor. On a given day, everyone marks a ballot and drops it in a box; the ballots are counted; and the one who got the most votes is the winner – simple as that – case closed!"

"Just a darn minute" objected Pinch, "It's not simple at all - matter of fact, it is very complicated and involves the very fundamentals of democracy, thus, many points of our constitution become involved." "Crap, expressed Tony, you jaybirds try to make a big deal about everything."

"Ok doubting Thomas, you asked for it so I'm prepared to discuss and analyze the subject of voting it the group is agreeable" rebutted Abe. "Yes" said Tony. "Let er rip" said Cowboy. And there was a smattering of Ok's from the rest of the crowd.

What democracy is all about is "Borders" and "Votes" began Abe. The borders are set (but not chiseled in stone) for towns, counties, states, and the nation. (and many other units) All the rules and governing take place inside one or several of these borders. Think about it. Democracy is government by the people - but decisions are made by people within certain borders. That is what arguments about States' rights vs. Federal rights, etc. are all about. The trend for the past hundred or more years has been toward Federal rights. We have yielded more and more power to the federal government. As a consequence, once politicians are elected or appointed to national office, they wield an immense amount of power and become God like in their thinking. I asked a Senator once why he didn't ask his constituents how they wanted him to vote on a particular issue - he said "I don't give a darn how they think or what they want - they elected me to use my own judgment when it came to voting - if they don't like what I do, they can vote for my opponent next election." Incidentally, he voted the way the lobbyist paid him to vote - and the voters promptly forgot about it and re-elected him the next election.

Professor said, "Since voting is so important and since we have made so much advances in technology - isn't it time that we try to improve how we vote? Most everyone nodded in the affirmative." "Ok then, lets vote ourselves on the following issues and discuss them as we go" "There are 7 of us here today and majority will govern."

The issues are -

1. Who should make the <u>rules</u> about the voting process?

      a. National level
        1. Congress
        2. Senate
        3. The President
        4. The electorate (voters)
      b. State level
      c. County level
      d. Town or city level

Hasn't this already been decided? Questioned Tony. "I thought it was covered by the constitution" The constitution states "majority" rules except for certain issues (impeachment, etc.) which require a 2/3 vote. It doesn't spell out how to vote. Today, the "How to vote" has been delegated to the state governments. But this is beside the point - we are taking a straw poll to decide if we should make changes to improve the voting process.

Lets vote -

    a. National level - Yes - 4 hands went up No - 3 hands
    b. State level -   Yes - 1 hand   No - 6 hands
    c. County level - Yes - 1 hand   No - 6 hands
    d. Town level -   Yes - 1 hand   No - 6 hands

All right, the majority thinks the <u>border</u> should be the

nation. That is what I expected. Everybody thinks big

daddy in Washington can solve all our problems. Let's

decide which big daddy can fix us up on this one - time

to vote -

    a. Congress -   Yes - 1 No - 6
    b. Senate -   Yes - 1 No - 6
    c. President -   Yes - 0 No - 7
    d. Voters -   Yes - 5 No - 2

How about -
    All the above   Yes - 7 No - 0

"So - you think it should be treated like an amendment

to the constitution? That is, hammered out in congress,

and the senate, then signed by the President. Then voted

on by the electorate? "Asked Lester. "You bet" responded Abe.

Let's get down to some of the nitty - gritty issues in voting - ok?

1. Who should be allowed to vote?

    a. Only U.S. citizens - Yes - 7   No - 0
    b. All U.S. residents - Yes - 0   No - 7

    Next -
    a. U.S. Citizens
        1. 21 years old or older - Yes - 1   No - 0
        2. 18 years old or older - Yes - 6   No - 0

2. Should anyone <u>not</u> be allowed to vote? Yes 6 No 0

    a. Convicted criminals - Yes - 5 No - 2
    b. Politicians and their employees - Yes - 3 No - 4

3. What language should be used on the ballots?

    a. English only   - Yes - 6   No - 1
    b. English and Spanish - Yes - 1 No - 6
    c. Other - Yes 0 No 7

4. What hours should the polls be open?

    a. 7am to 6pm - each time zone - Yes - 2 No - 5
    b. 7am Pacific time zone to 6pm Eastern time zone
        (or 1000 to 1600 Greenwich mean time) - Yes -
5 No - 2

5. What day of the week should National elections by

held on -

    Saturday   - 6 to 1

6. Should the mechanics, etc. of the voting process by
<u>standardized</u> throughout the nation?

    Yes 7   -   No 0

7. Can we and should we rely on modern technology
(specifically computers and electronics) 100% in
   the voting process?

    Yes 6   -   No 1

8. Should we continue the voter registration process?

    Yes 3   -   No 4

9. Without the registration process - how do you
control who votes?

    *With electronics   Yes 6 - No 1

10. Who should monitor the voting process?

     *Political party representatives   Yes 5 - No 2
     *Paid govt. employees   Yes 1 - No 6
     *Police Yes 1 - No 6

11. Should we eliminate the electoral college?

     Yes 6 - No 1

Abe asked - "any other thoughts?"

Cowboy responded. "One thing that always bothers me when I vote is - I don't know a darn thing about the <u>lower</u> level candidates - particularly in state and local elections. Also, when we are asked to vote on such things as bond issues etc. - I don't know much about it - especially how much it will cost <u>me</u>." "What I'm driving at is - the present information distribution system doesn't work very well and I think there should be changes made."

"I have a solution for that "chimed in Tony. "What is it?" asked Professor. "Why don't we require the newspaper to publish a copy of the ballot along with (a) candidate pictures and profiles (b) candidate score card and (c) complete discussion of anything on the ballot."

"Yes, and the newspapers always give you a list of who they recommend you vote for - just before the election" said Cowboy - who added "and that ain't right."

"They do most of that already" pointed out Stewart. "Besides, who is going to pay for this?"

"This bunch is just like the American public" griped Tony. "Every time we try to come up with a positive solution for a problem, there is always someone who tries to "Shoot you down" when you make a suggestion."

"I wish we had a blackboard and chalk so I could show you what I'm suggesting" Said Abe. "Here's a tablet and pen" offered Tony. "Write it down and pass it

around why don't you."

Abe immediately began writing and composed the

following:

(1) Ballot:

```
┌─────────────────────────┐
│                         │
│                         │
│                         │
│                         │
│                         │
│                         │
│                         │
│         Sample          │
│         Ballot          │
└─────────────────────────┘
```

(2) Voting instructions:

(To be written <u>after</u> we decide on all the voting issues set forth above).

(3) Candidate Profile

Name _____

Resident
Address

_____

Occupation

_____
Picture

AFE _____

Family _____   Questionnaire Score _____

Education _____   Military

Experience _____

Elected Office   Arrest Record _____
Experience _____

Voting score card _____
                                         _____
                                         Church Affiliation

Appx. Net Worth _____

(4) Other items on the ballot

    * Summary Description _____

    * Estimated amount spent (per voter) _____

    * Pro - Summary

    * Con Summary

The newspaper would be "paid" for this public service by tax credits - say $1 per unit of circulation.

When he completed the example - he handed it to Tony. Tony read it and passed it to Cletus. As each person read it they scowled, smiled, and frowned - obviously there was going to be more discussion. Lester broke the silence with "You can't force people to divulge all this information - it's discrimination!"

"Heck fire" exclaimed Abe, "Voting itself is discrimination personified - what's wrong with discrimination?"

"Well, somebody would file a lawsuit and it would end up at the Supreme Court - and they would rule that it is discrimination." "That's what's wrong." snapped Pinch.

"Hump the Supreme Court" rebutted Abe. "That's something else we need to discuss and get that situation straightened out."

"Not today" Ruled out Cowboy. Let's vote on Abe's suggestion now - all is favor - 4 hands; up opposed - 3 hands.

"One thing that bothers me, spoke up Ace, is that the government collects money from us taxpayers and turns right around and flat out gives it to the politicians for their "Campaigns". Heck, I'll bet most of them just stuff it in their pocket and never spend it" Why don't we cut out that robbery?"

"Let's vote" said Cowboy. Leave it alone? Yes 5 No 2

(The thought of most based on murmurs in the room was - it ain't robbery if you voluntary give it to them - if you don't agree with it - mark the No ☐ on the tax return).

"Any more thoughts? Inquired Professor. Silence. Well, that about wraps up the subject of voting so - "Let's play dominos."

"Hold your horses! demanded Pinch. I don't think we hardly scratched the surface on the voting issues. We kind of decided that it could be done and controlled in the future by electronics - but we didn't get into any of the details. In my opinion, we're relying entirely too much on those darn computers and they are going to become the ruination of this nation".

"Don't get so hot and bothered Pinch - we aren't going to be able to solve all the problems of the world with this little group of old farts assembled here - but we can talk about them" cautioned Abe. What I think should happen would be similar to how the government buys military aircraft for example. First, they take bids for the development of a new airplane. After they accept a prototype, they then take bids for the actual manufacture and supply of aircraft."

"For this exercise, the government would prepare the specs (expectations) of the project and put the project up for bid. The many brain trusts, high tech companies, think tanks, etc. would submit bids. The bidder would get a development contract - or better yet, they might award two or three contracts. Then when the contracts were completed, they would go through the same process for the manufacture and implementation."

Knowing just enough about current electronic technology to be dangerous, I assume that most of them would come up with somewhat as follows:

(1) Voter - established a "fool proof" method of positive identification.

*Could be "micro chip" implants
*Could be "tattoos"
*Could be some sort of scanning
   technique (eyes, finger prints, navels,?)
*Could rely on the present "voter registration" process

This step is critical in the "control" process.

(2) Voting mechanism - this is the "tool" to be used for voting. It could be -

*Punched cards
*Key boards
*Vocal input
*Touching screens
*Mind reading

(Threw that last one in the scare you) there is little doubt that everyone would propose the use of computers as the future tool for voting - it just makes sense) and we already have the technologies (outlined above) available for "input" to the computers.

(3) Compiling the vote - this is the method of counting the votes. It could be done very easily by electronic means, including -

```
  *Computers networked -
   *National network
   *State network
   *Other network
 *Individual computer printouts - results
```

transmitted to national assembly point by phone, fax, etc.

If we agreed to rely on electronics solely for voting, it makes no sense to maintain the electoral college so we might as well dispense with it. And of course, the system must have all available protective and safety features - else, some young computer "Geek" might break in and control the results of an election.

My own idea is that the following networks be set up -

    *State network
    *Quadrant (national) network
    *National network

There would be a vote auditor at each network who would be required to "Certify" the results before they could be passed up to the next network level. <u>Absolutely</u> <u>no</u> results would be given to the press until <u>after</u> the polls close and results are certified.

"Now let's get on with dominos" concluded Abe.

CHAPTER 17

YOU CAN FOOL ALL OF THE PEOPLE

SOME OF THE TIME.......

It was a hot July morning as the group gathered for its regular session of dominos and other important matters - including gossip. Abe had overslept and didn't get the air conditioner turned on early and it was hotter than a seduced sheep in a jalapeño patch in the close quarters of the "domino parlor." Bulldog had brought a sack of ice and a jug of sweetened tea and most everyone had opted for iced tea instead of coffee this morning.

Professor started the talk fest by "I woke up this morning with a crazy idea on my mind - why are the American public so darn stupid? The expression - you can fool all of the people some of the time and some of the people all of the time - but you can't fool all of the people all of the time (or something like that) kept running through my mind. I don't know who said that but I was doubting its accuracy. It appears to me that the Washington bunch has got it down pat - they fool the American public all of the time. nobody seems to question anything anymore and few seem to even give a darn.

Wal Professor, to answer one of your concerns - the expression "you can fool all of the people some of the time, and some of the people all of the time" is credited to Abraham Lincoln. Who later added "But you can't fool all of the people all of the time". But - what set you off?" "Who pulled your chain?" asked Abe.

"By gawd, spoke up Cowboy, Bush sending our soldiers overseas to Iraq set me off. I know he is lying through his teeth to us about the reasons for doing such a stupid thing. But nobody challenges him. When are we going to wake up and do something?

"Probably never" drawled Abe. Political corruption and all the related sins have been going on since the very beginning of the United States - and long before that in the rest of the world. That's just the way that it is with human beings. There is always going to be some who will do anything to accumulate wealth - even murder their fellow man.

"But how do they fool everyone?" Asked Cowboy.

"Aw heck, - that ain't too hard to do - providing you got plenty of money' responded Abe. It's called "Brainwashing" and it works something like this-

1. First you run up the flag and create a patriotic issue - someone is endangering the good ole U.S. of A". In this

latest fiasco - Bush convinced everyone that the "terrorist" were out to destroy us - he had the 9-11 destruction of the World Trade Center to work with. Prior to that, his old man claimed Saddam Hussein was after us cause he had invaded Kuwait." And before that, Nixon had the red menace - communism to work with. If you study our history it has always been some "danger to the flag" that made the brainwash work.

2. Second, you have to hammer away at the public with the same theme over a relatively long period of time. This is done by controlling the news media which is step 3. In fact, there are only 16 news sources to control.

The next step is control of the legal system. Since most judges are appointed particularly the supreme court judges - it ain't hard to figure that one out. Remember how ole Franklin D. Roosevelt loaded up the supreme court with his puppets after he unloaded his "new deal" on us.

And finally, you buy off the influential columnist and commentators who then become "Spokesman for the administration."

"I don't believe that bull crap" said Cletus. "It might work in Germany or someplace like that - but not in the good ole U.S.A."

"If you are referring to Hitler, said Abe, that ain't the way he did it. He just used force and scared the beans out of anyone who opposed him. But back to my point - take a look at just a few of the major

trick screwing the American public has received the past 50 years or so:

* Kent State   *Pentagon papers   *Iraq I
*Chappaquiddick
*Mylas   *Assinations (K,K,&K) *Iraq II
*Pueblo incident
*Communism   *Watergate
*Gulf of Tonkin
*Vietnam

CHAPTER 18

THE THIRD PARTY - BULL MOOSE?

Abe decided to start the February meeting of the domino club off with a bang so as soon as everyone had gotten their cup of coffee and were settling in he stood up and asked "How many of you died in the wool, donkey riding democrats? Three hands went up.

Next he asked "How many of you are elephant poop scooping republicans? Three other hands went up.

Is it safe to assume then that you other three (1) don't give a darn either way (2) vote for the man instead of the party, or think you are (3) independents.

The point I would like to make today is this "This country needs a third political party to represent the voters who are not committed to the Democratic or Republican parties." stressed Abe.

In any election, approximately 1/3 of the voters pull the straight donkey (democrat) lever and another 1/3 pull the straight elephant (republican) lever. The other 1/3 vote according to how they were persuaded by the millions of dollars worth of bull poop that was flung at them during the pre-election campaigns.

I believe there is a strong base of voters who still feel strongly about the fundamental (God, country, mother, apple pie, fair play, individual freedom, etc.) upon which this nation was built.

Therefore, I think this new political party's platform should be based upon those fundamentals - and stick to it. No middle of the road bottle assing around.

"I think you have a good idea there governor - what do you propose to name this third party? Spoke up Ace.

"Really haven't settled on a name yet," answered Abe. Some of the names I have been kicking around include:

*Freedom
*Bull Moose
*Minute man

Freedom because the fundamental belief of our nation is <u>Freedom</u>. Bull Moose because that was a third party (even hear of Theodore Roosevelt) in the 19th Century. And minute man because that is what our founding fathers were called. I'm sure each of you can think of other names which are just as appropriate.

"How about enterprise?" asked Pinch. "Then is a nation that beliefs strongly in free enterprise."

"I like Longhorn or maybe Lone Star" interrupted Professor.

"Neither of those will fly" responded Abe. They are pure Texan and we never stop to think, or admit, that the rest of the U.S.A. don't think like us or even care for us. They are jealous of us when you get right down to the short hair.

"Hey fellers, I just thought of the perfect name "Spoke up Geek" in an excited voice.

"Wal, let us in on it then" said Abe.

"The 9-11 party" beamed Geek as he spoke.

"I'll admit that is a timely name but I don't think it would pass the test of time" flatly argued Cowboy. The nation is in an uproar over a few radicals who stole some airplanes and committed suicide but took a bunch of good folk with them on September 11, 2001. That date 9-11 sort of became a battle cry and pulled the nation together - but I suspect that ten years from now, maybe less, it won't have much meaning to the majority of folks. For example, does "12-7" or "remember pearl harbor" receive much attention today. Heck no - we are also a forgiving and forgetting nation.

It appears to me that deciding on a name is the least of the problems if you wish to start another political party" wisely injected Abe. "That's right said Cowboy, our memories are about as short as our talley wackers." "Don't you boys remember a couple of years back when that little banty rooster - Ross Perot - tried to get a third party going down in Dallas, - and finally gave up. Heck, he's got so much money, he could stack it up in Dallas, climb up on top of it and see us up here in Bugscuffle. I spec he figured that big pile of money would disappear before he got a third party going strong enough to replenish it. Like most everything, in the final analysis it comes down to money. " "Where are we going to get the money to start your party?" Abe concluded.

"You are absolutely right Abe "stated Pinch.   This project would take a heck of a big wad of cash. Maybe the "seed" money could come from a grant - either government or private. Once it got rolling it would need substantial political contributions to keep it going.

Abe said "I've already started preparing a grant request. If the money comes through we can be the brain trust that builds the skeleton and gets the ball rolling. Then we can farm the rest out to other "think tanks" to put the flesh on the bones.

I even called Mr. Perot to see if he wanted to help out - didn't get to talk to him but did leave him a message - so far, haven't heard back from him."

CHAPTER 19

THE DEREGULATION FIASCO

As the group gathered for its regular session of domino playing, gossip, and enlightment on a blustery winter day in late February, Lester said "I've got a question to toss out at this august body this morning."

Abe said. "Settle down fellers and listen. Lester has a question for us this morning that seems to be troubling him something fierce. (Lester had a troubled look on his usual friendly face). Ok Lester, what is your question?"

Lester said, I got a call last Tuesday or Wednesday, can't remember which, from a feller who said he represented some "energy" company, that I had never heard of, who was trying to sell me "power." I asked him what kind of power he was peddling and he said electricity. I told him I already had all the electricity I needed but he was persistent - said he <u>guaranteed</u> to reduce my electric bill by 20%.

That got my attention - my light bill runs over $100 a month on average and a $240 annual saving is something to think about. I took down his number - one of them 800 numbers - and told him I would think about it and call him back. My question then is "should I change electric companies and is this a real deal?"

Professor chuckled and said "Welcome to the post Reaganomics era of deregulation. I'm surprised you haven't already had calls about switching telephone service too. My wife has mentioned getting such calls but I've already switched telephone companies - several times. Every time I get a check from one of them (AT&T, SBC, MCI, etc.) I cash it and then I'm automatically switched - although it takes months to get the screwed up bills straightened out. I don't understand what's going on. When I changed phone companies, the new company didn't come out and set new poles and run a new line to the house - matter of fact, nothing happened."

"Join the crowd said Tony. I don' t think anybody knows what the heck is going on anymore." Can anybody in this brain trust explain it to us?"

"I'll try, volunteered Abe. Back in the infancy of this nation several very large companies sprung up and took over markets. They monopolized the markets and that was bad, they literally could name their own price." So the government got busy and started breaking them up through legislation (antitrust legislation).

Finally, someone got wise and spoke up saying "not all monopolies are bad - some make a lot of sense." For example, providers of electricity. It took millions of dollars to build the generating plants and the power lines - let alone individual home installations. Can you imagine what Dallas would be like if it was served by five electric companies - each with its own generating plants and power lines that birds couldn't fly in and out of the city. There would be such a scrambling for fuel that the price of fuel would go sky high - and so would the cost of electricity. Some of the companies would not make it and would go bankrupt. It would be a very wasteful thing. So they finally decided to let one company in the market have it all - but the price to the customer along with other things would be <u>regulated</u>.

This process served the nation well (although not perfectly) for a couple of hundred years. Then we elect a movie actor as president and he comes up with his own economic rules (called Reaganomics) and sets about lifting the regulations on regulated companies. But Ronnie had help - ever hear of Newt Gingich and Phil Gramm. This was stupid and darn near chaotic in my view. Look at the screwed up mess we now have in the following industries that were once regulated:

(a) Communications (telephone and tv)
(b) Electric utilities
(c) Airlines
(d) Banking

The way deregulation was done was somewhat as follows:

The government crammed down the throats of the regulated companies a requirement that they <u>sell</u> product to another company at (at or below) cost if the buyer bought in large quantity. Then, they rubbed salt in the wound and said "By the way, you also must do the customer accounting for them." Cute huh?

The end result was a proliferation of <u>marketing</u> companies lying like dogs to the public. "Heck fire, spoke up Tony, deregulation sucks."

"Well, some of it may be academic at this point, wisely said Abe, we are very rapidly headed toward <u>wireless</u> communications and perhaps even <u>wireless</u> power - it is possible that an economic way will be found to capture the sun power on small household units."

"But what about travel, "asked Cowboy."

"Well, high speed trains make a lot more sense than airplanes for continental travel and higher speed ships make more sense for crossing the ocean - with supersonic aircraft as to alternative for the fools in such a darn hurry.

Worldwide monopolies should be set up and regulated for inter-continental travel," added Abe.

"There is another problem that sort of goes hand in hand with regulation" said Ace - and that is the effect or on our economy, etc. By the environmentalists. I chuckle when I hear advertising by the fake electric utility companies trying to sell you clean or green electricity. They think we are idiots. Once electricity gets on a power line it is just electricity - there is no way to distinguish how it was produced - coal, wind, water, etc!

Do we realize that millions (maybe billions) of wind generating machines have been built - you see them all over Texas - and most don't produce any electricity for us. They aren't connected to the transmission lines. They were built with tax credits, subsides, etc. and the speculators who built them <u>assumed</u> the power generating companies would build transmission lines to them to get the electricity.

The power companies, after the Barnett shale was tapped, said no way - we can build gas fired generators cheaper. Great planning - huh?

CHAPTER 20

THE HISTORY OF AUDITING

At the next session of the fraternity, Tony brought a copy of the Jacksboro Bugle (newspaper) and laid it on the domino table with the glaring headlines exposed "Enron Collapses - Arthur Anderson To Blame." Everyone had heard about it of course - it had dominated the news for days.

Tony said, "Pinch, you were a C.P.A. before you retired weren't you? What do you have to say about all this?

"Well, said Pinch, if I tried to explain what happened and give my opinion on how and why it happened - it would take the rest of the day and most of tomorrow." Tony said." Fine with me - I can forego dominos for a day or so if you are willing to explain that fiasco. Except for Geek, everyone else expressed the same view.

To begin with - let's clear the air about what happened. Enron was a public company and its management ranks contained a few greedy men who went bad - they are, in fact, criminals - they committed crimes.

On the other hand, Arthur Anderson did some stupid things and went along with Enron probably for the same reason - greed.

The reasons for both mistakes can be found in the past if one takes the time to analyze the past and learn its lessons.

Let's take a few minutes and look at Enron. The company was built on smoke and mirrors - much the same as most of the new companies started in the U.S.A. since World War II. It really didn't produce anything. It was a marketing creation which wiggled and wormed its way through the proliferation on legislation coming out of Washington - particularly de-regulation. Almost all the manufacturing is slipping away to the third world countries and this will eventually be the death of the U.S. capitalistic society. Enron <u>marketed</u> energy.

The accounting profession is the youngest of the recognized professions - yet it has much in common with the oldest of the professions. It performs services for fees. There are many misconceptions about the accounting profession - especially the audit services it provides. Many still believe (including some CPA's I know) that a "clean" audit opinion on a set of financial statements is a <u>guarantee</u> that everything is hunky dory. This simply is not true - <u>read</u> the audit report!

The simple fact is - people do not make investment decisions based solely on the audit report. But that is another subject which would take a book to explain. They merely look to the auditor as another scapegoat when things don't work out - and sue him. Lawyers always look for "deep pockets."

When I started in the accounting professional we had one, yes one, official published pronouncement which supported what was called generally accepted accounting principles (GAAP). That document was ARB (Accounting Research Bulletin) No. 63 and it dealt principally with defense contracts (World War II you know) GAAP really was what you learned from Finney & Miller (acct. textbook). Auditors relied heavily on a solid audit of the balance sheet. (It was easier to verify in the limited time available).

Furthermore, all accountants knew what a balance sheet was - what it was supposed to look like - and how you checked it out.

The left side represented assets and assets were stuff the entity <u>owned</u>. These assets were shown at what they <u>cost</u>. Starting at the top, they were shown in the order or how they would spin through the cash cycle. Those that would make it back to cash within a year were called current assets - all others were noncurrent. Duh!

The right side represented liabilities and equity. Liabilities were debts or what the entity owed. Whatever remained mathematically when you subtracted the liabilities from the assets was called equity. Did I say <u>worth</u> - no, I said equity. Because the balance sheet was represented by <u>historical</u> costs, there was no way in heck to show "worth" - and there still isn't. There is an ongoing change in value and the balance sheet represented a finite point in time - it changed the very next instant.

There were, and are, many things of value not recorded as assets. These things include excellent people (management, workers, etc.) and products (Gillette razors, Colgate tooth paste, etc.). Also, many assets may have appreciated in value. (i.e. - land, buildings, etc.)

On the other hand, there were many things which might have detracted from value which were not always recorded. And these little jewels have always given auditors fits. We developed what was called the conservative approach. This approach said simply, if you could prove that an asset had diminished in value (from its historical cost basis) - you wrote it down to its (then "current value." If you discovered a liability not recorded

- you recorded it - even (and often) at ('guest mated amounts."

There were four basic things you did to <u>audit</u> a balance sheet.

      1. Use your senses - touch it, kick it, feel it, look at it.
      2. Go to a source outside the entity and have them tell you about it (confirm it).
      3. Look at the documents and do the math (prepaid assets, accrued expenses, etc.).
      4. Use as much "hindsight" as possible.

In theory then, if you were satisfied with the balance sheets at the frontend and backend of the <u>period</u> of time covered by the statement of operations - the difference between the beginning equity and ending equity was profit (if equity increased) or (loss) (if equity decreased), your major concern then was in <u>classifications</u>.

We got along with this approach for a few years but along came a, screw up or two in the public company environment and the Securities and Exchange Commission (SEC) started demanding more rules.

There was implied threat from congress to regulate the accounting profession.

The accounting profession responded and set up the Accounting Principles Board and they started cranking out rules and we started becoming a "cookbook" profession. Audit files began getting crammed full and choked with programs and checklist. Those who could memorize the rules and quote Chapter and verse became known as the audit experts. And others got into the rule making process -

*The Audit Standards Board
*Govt. Accounting

The area which received the most attention from the rule makers in the ensuing years was not the actual recording of transactions - rather; it was the discussion about what had been (how, and why) recorded or not recorded and other information which the rule makers thought the reader of the financials needed to know. This disclosure information was presented as footnotes to the financial statements. A good footnote writer was one who could speak with a forked tongue. Much time was spent writing and re-writing those footnotes and many were not fully understood by the auditors - much less the poor unsophisticated investors.

The accountants were not entirely to blame for most of the "required" disclosure. Much of it was the result of pressure from the SEC. (and who checked or the SEC - what made them so expert? don't know).

By 1992 we must have had a half zillion rules. Then, the crap hit the fan again. There were some more major screw ups on public company audits and the companies bellied up. A couple of senators (Moss from Michigan) and (Metcalf from Ohio) decided it was time for the Federal Government to take over and straighten things out in the accounting profession.

However, before they succeeded the accountants countered with the Financial Accounting Standards Board (FASB). This self serving board contained accountants and non accountants and was charged with rule making on a going forward basis. Moss and Metcalf backed off and we charged forward into the FASB) era - same old song - just new verses.

Early in this era it appeared that FASB - might finally get it right. They started a project called "Accounting Postulates" which was going to write the Bible and explain, in greater detail, what I just got through telling you about the early balance sheet approach to audits.

What was even better was - they would write two bibles - the big GAAP version for public companies and the little GAAP version for everybody else. But for whatever reason, these projects were abandoned and they jumped back into Betty Crocker - trying to write a new recipe for anything <u>new</u> that appeared on the horizon.

In the meantime, the use of computers was exploding and things were getting faster and faster. It took a heck of a stout computer just to hold a reference list of all the rules and if you had a copy of everything published, you needed a good sized building just to house your library.

In the meantime, the U.S. economy was changing drastically. Manufacturing was rapidly moving to the third world. Washington was deregulating everything. Whole new industries were springing up and investors went gambling crazy, if you think they were paying any attention to financial statements and audit reports when they were buying stocks like the following;

Company	Stock Price	Assets	Liab	Equity	Share Book Value
Sky High	$10.00	$11 mil	$12 mil	($1 mil)	($1)
Buy Me Now	2.00	26 mil	40 mil	($14 mil)	(14)

The broker says after the "investor" buys this stock-

"Now let me show you a picture of a bridge I have for sale."

Then the crap hits the fan again - Enron: (Notice how this is becoming cyclical.) Again, there is an outcry from Washington - regulate the auditors. But first, let's put the cuffs on management. They are now required to put their names on the line on reports filed with the SEC. and who the heck knows what is to follow. All I know, is this - there was never a collection of folks more <u>unethical</u>, greedy, and <u>unfit</u> to make rules than the boys in Washington.

If you really want to present information to investors that <u>might</u> help them make more informed investment decisions - require periodic reports containing the following:

1. Financial statements
2. Management representation
3. Auditors opinion
4. Lawyers representation
5. Report prepared by financial analysis
6. Products (or services) evaluation
7. Directors certification

Now - that gives the lawyers a whole bunch of new folks to sue when the train jumps the track.

CHAPTER 21

HOW DO YOU PROTECT THE INVESTORS?

It had been a heck of a week on wall street. The Enron scandal had broken and the Dow Jones averages had dropped another 900 points.

Most of the group had assembled and Pinch said. "They ought to hang that Enron bunch - including those crooked CPA's at Arthur Anderson" exclaimed Tony. Most everyone seemed to be in agreement. Cowboy piped up "Pinch, I've been thinking about what you told us last week and I'm more confused than ever."

"Sure" responded Pinch. I admit it's very complicated but if you really want it explained - I would be happy to spend the rest of the day discussing it.

"Tell you what - lets vote on it" said Abe. They voted and everyone wanted to hear more and Abe added "Tell us how you would go about protecting investors in the future." "Ok" said Lester, pay attention cause I'm only going through this exercise this time. If you don't understand something - stop me and ask questions. I'm going to assume you all know darn little about financial statements, audits, wall street, investing, regulations/regulators, etc. Even though I expect that some of you know a heck of a lot more than I about some of the subjects.

"Before I commence this sermon, let me ask a few questions - raise your hands to respond." said Pinch.

1. How many of you have bought common stocks?(5 hands raised).
2. How many of you read the financial statements, including the auditors opinion, <u>before</u> you bought the stock? (1 hand raised).

3. Very interesting -   did you base your decision to purchase the stock on your reading of the financial statements? Tony said no.

4. Then, why did you buy the stock? Tony responded, cause the stock broker said it was a "Good buy" "I see" said Pinch.

5. Did you understand the financial statements? "Not really" responded Tony.

"Now, let's see what we just learned from this exercise." said Pinch.   First - very few investors rely on the company's financial statements and/or the auditors' opinion for investment decisions. Sad - but true. Second - very few people (investors or otherwise) understand financial statements and even fewer understand the auditors' role.

Then, you may ask "Who really uses the financial statements and auditors opinions? Answer - regulators and litigators. I'll explain this in more detail as we progress. But first, let's get in a lesson while the subject is fresh. I'm going to give you the basics on financial

212

statements and the auditors opinion - what they are and what they are not.

Financial Statements - are the recorded history of the entity they represent. They consist of (a) balance sheet (b) profit and loss statement (c) cash flow statement, and (d) disclosure footnotes. Amounts shown are in historical cost dollars.

The balance sheet shows what the entity owns at a point in time (called assets), what it owes at a point in time (called liabilities), and the difference between the two (called equity). Additional explanatory information about the balance sheet is contained in the footnote disclosures. Warning - the balance sheet does not show what the company is "worth" or "value". Further, by the time you read the balance sheet - most of the amounts will have changed - assuming the date on the balance sheet was December 31, 2001 - those numbers were only half way accurate as the clock struck 12 on December 31st. They changed at 12:<u>01</u> and every second thereafter.

The profit and loss statement, on the other hand, shows the dollar amounts of the transactions the company entered into during a <u>period</u> of time - i.e. from one balance sheet to the next. It reflects the <u>results</u> of its operations and shows revenue (what it sold or earned) and costs and expenses (what it spent or committed to). If revenue is greater than expenses - a <u>profit</u> results. If the reverse - it's a loss much effort is spent trying to <u>match</u> costs and expenses with revenues so you get the correct amounts in the right "time frames". The final results (the ole "bottom line") must equal the change in equity on the beginning balance sheet and the ending balance sheet.

The so called "cash flow statement" shows the components of changes in cash from one balance sheet to the next. It can be confusing to read and understand because of the way it is sometimes presented. This is caused by accrual accounting and the fact that cash flows through both the balance sheet accounts and the operating accounts.

"Hold on there partner" interrupted Cowboy. You're talking Chinese or something or another now and I don't understand what the heck you're talking about. Give me an illustration.

"Good" said Pinch. I'm glad someone is paying attention.

Let's take Bob's feed store as an example. Let's then look at what happens during the year. Let's assume he buys 500 fifty pound sacks of cow feed from the feed mill at $5 a sack. He owed the mill $2,000 at the beginning of the cycle (year) and had 100 sacks of feed on hand at the beginning of the year also. (Assume his cost of those 100 sacks was $4 a sack. Next, assume he sold 200 sacks at $7 a sack for cash money and 150 sacks at $8 a sack on credit and had not collected for it at the end of the cycle (year). Assume he paid the mill the $2,000 he owed at the beginning of the year plus $1,500 more on the purchase of the 500 sacks (cost $2,500) in other words, he still owed the mill $1,000 at year end.

Let's see how the numbers appear on the basic financial statements: (He produced a black board and chalk and wrote)

Balance Sheet			Operating Statement	
Assets	Beginning	Ending	Sales	$2,600
Cash	$3,000	$ 900	Cost	1,650
Accounts rec.	-0-	1,200	Profit	$ 950
Inventory	400	1,250		
Liabilities				
Accounts				
payable	(2,000)	(1,000)		

"Whoa Stop right there interrupted Cowboy. How can you say the cost was only $1,650? I've been writing the numbers down and I came up with $2,500 as what he spent - that's his real <u>cost</u>. You said yourself he bought 500 sacks at $5 a sack and that equals $2,500 - any way you figure it."

"Naw, that ain't right dummy" said Professor. He still owned 150   sacks at the end of the year didn't he. That's what that inventory asset is. You got to subtract $1,250 from your $2,500 to get his true cost - and that leaves $1,250 as cost - wait a minute - he shows $1,650 as cost -

something ain't right. No wonder you CPA's are in hot water - you can't even add or subtract.

"Aw crap - how did I let myself get trapped into trying to explain this complicated mess to a bunch of knuckleheads like you." Let me digress for a minute and throw out some of the complications in accounting that crop up in this relatively simple illustration.

First - accounting has rules that have been developed over the years that must be followed. Without them, there would be shor nuff chaos. These rules are called generally accepted accounting principles usually referred to as "GAAP". Some of these rules have options. This brings up another question "who should select the option?" It has long been established by law that the financial statements are the responsibility of the entity - therefore, whoever represents the entity (usually "management" gets to select the option. This means they must use good judgment.

Now, back to our illustration. The rules and options in our simple illustration are as follows:

Balance sheet

Inventory - Inventory should be valued at cost. However, there are options as to the computations, the option valuation methods (calculations) are called -

First in - first out - (FI-FO) - basically, this assumes you keep the "fresh" stuff in the warehouse and ship out the oldest stuff. In our illustration, the 350 sacks sold would have been the 100 "old" sacks in beginning inventory plus 250 sacks of the 500 "new" sacks he bought. The ending inventory would be the balance of the new sacks or 250 sacks which cost $5 each - thus

$1,250 in inventory.   This is the method used in my illustration.

Last in - first out (LI-FO) - this assumes you ship the "fresh" stuff (or the customer picks it up) and the oldest stuff is left in inventory. Under this option, the 250 sacks in ending inventory would have consisted of -

150 sacks of new stuff @ $5	$ 750
100 sacks of old stuff @ $4	400
Inventory	$1,150

Average - this assumed you just throw everything in the put and compute the "average" unit price - in this case it would be -

100 sacks @ $4	$ 400	
500 sacks @ $5	2,500	
600	$2,900	$2,900 ÷ 6 = $4.83

Ending inventory - 250 sacks @ $4.83 = $1,207.50

There are even more methods but I'll not get into them - this should be sufficient to illustrate the point.

"Well I'll be darned" injected Cowboy, now I see why some folks say CPA's are slick with the numbers and can get you about any answer you want."

"That is not true" argued Pinch, and I resent such remarks. All the CPA's I know are very honest and of extremely high morals and integrity. Admittedly, they are just folks, like us, and occasionally a rotten apple turns up in the barrel. But they do a good job of policing their ranks and get rid of the bad apples in a hurry.

"I'm beginning to get the hang of this inventory business said Geek, but what about cost?"

If you understand inventory, then cost is simple. It is merely what we took out (relieved from) inventory. Let's go back to the inventory illustrations:

FIFO - We "put in" and "took out" the following:

Quantity	Unit Cost	Put In	Sacks	Took out (cost)	Sacks	Balance
FIFO -						
100 sacks	$4	$ 400	100	$ 400		-
500 sacks	$5	2,500	(250)	1,250	250	1,250
600 Totals		$2,900	350	$1,650	250	$ 1,250
LIFO -						
100 sacks		$ 400	-	$ -	100	400
500 sacks		2,500	350	1,750	150	750
600 Totals		$2,900	350	$1,750	250	$1,150
Average						
100 sacks		$ 400				
500 sacks		2,500				
600 ($4.83)		$2,900	350	$1,692	250	$1,207

"Oh yeah said Geek That's pretty slick - I see how it works now". But what if a rat chewed a hole in two or three sacks of your inventory. I know that happens. Rats are bad around a feed store. And that old tom cat over at Bob's store is too darn lazy to catch a rat.

"Wal Geek, that's a very good point but there ain't a heck of a lot new under the sun - particularly when it comes to accounting. The point you make comes under one of the very basic rules of reporting which is sometimes called "the foundation of <u>conservative</u> accounting (and reporting). The rule simply states - value (or show) assets at the <u>lower</u> of <u>cost</u> or market. In this case, the three damaged sacks might have a market value of .50¢ each. Therefore, the inventory would be reduced by appx. $14 - depending on the method. This is sometimes done with a <u>valuation</u> <u>reserve</u> account. Let's look at another number in our feed store example which may need adjusting. Any ideas as to which number I'm talking about?"

"Is it accounts payable?" meekly asked Tony. "How could that be" jumped in Cowboy. Why heck, old Bob has been known to stiff a creditor or two in the past - he might of got pissed off at the mill for raising the price (from $4 to $5 a sack) on him and he ain't going to pay them.

"More" than likely it's the feller that old Bob shafted when he sold him that feed on the credit for $1 more than his cash sale. He probably found out how old Bob shafted him and he ain't going to pay unless he just has to or unless old Bob adjusted his bill " volunteered Bulldog. "Exactly right" praised Pinch. Now the judgment comes in - how much do you think the customer will <u>actually</u>

pay?" "I'd say maybe $7 a sack - same as the cash sale"

responded Billy.   That's as good a <u>guess</u> as any (and

judgment quite often is no more than an educated guess)

so let's set up a <u>valuation</u> adjustment for $150 (150 sacks

x $1). This valuation reserve is normally called "reserve

for bad debts."

"That's purty neat spoke up Professor - maybe CPA's

ain't so dumb after all."

"Thanks. Thanks a heap" answered Pinch.

"If the company, or its management , is responsible for

the financial statements, what the heck do the auditors do

and what is their responsibility? Asked Professor. "They

got to be responsible for something, else they wouldn't be

ponying up millions to settle some of the big lawsuits we

read about."

"A lawyer, particularly a litigator, would give you a different answer than what I'm going to explain" answered Pinch. So perhaps I should preface my comments with the phase "in my opinion." The auditor is responsible for expressing his <u>honest</u> opinion about the financial statements and to include any important information (usually disclosure stuff) in his report not containing in the financial statements which he feels the reader should be aware of. He is also responsible for conducting his audit in accordance with the auditor rules - called generally accepted auditing standards or "GAAS". The only thing in the report prepared by and signed only by the auditor is the auditors <u>opinion</u> - period.

"This is starting to sound like an army lecture the way you keep tossing out them acronyms" noted Ace. "Tell us, in simple terms, what an audit really is and what the rules are." "Also, what do you think makes a good auditor - and heh, heh, - are you one?"

"Those sound like loaded questions" responded Pinch, but I'll do my best to answer them.

First, let's tackle the audit itself." A good auditor puts himself in the place of the statement preparer and tries to gather sufficient facts in order to agree on disagree with the financial statements. In this process, there is no substitute for common -nee- uncommon sense, experience, and a good understanding of economics and business." Economic substance is the most critical factor in any issue.

Let's see what the auditor has available to do his job. I'll start with the balance sheet - the point in time statement. For certain balances, you can use your senses to check them out. It's somewhat like examining a used tractor you are contemplating buying - you can physically "kick the tires." For example - inventory. In our earlier discussion we said that Bob had 250 sacks of cow feed in his ending inventory. At December 31st (balance sheet date) you could have gone by Bob's feed store and physically counted the 250 sacks of feed. At that time you could also have inspected them and seen the three sacks that the rats had gotten into and made a notation of them. Later, you could have examined the invoices and checked out the math and pricing. You could have done these things but you didn't - that was Bob's responsibility. Your job is to be sure that Bob did it so you merely observed and "tested" what Bob did. But you still used your <u>senses</u> to check out this <u>tangible</u> asset.

And while you were there, you could have obtained a list of his property and equipment (fixed assets or depreciable assets) and looked them over and kicked a few tires" making note of anything out of the ordinarily. For example, you might see an old delivery truck out back with weeds growing up around it. Upon inquiry, you find that it is an old junker that won't run and was kept to pirate for parts - their new delivery truck is the same brand - a Ford. However, it is still on the depreciation schedule at a net book value (original cost less accumulated depreciation) of $5,000. You make a note of this and later propose an adjustment to write it down to "fair value" - remember - conservative accounting. By the way - in case you haven't figured it out - conservative accounting means it's ok to understate assets and to overstate liabilities - but the reverse is a no - no.

"Yeah, but suppose old Bob don't agree with you - he won't make your adjustment" said Cowboy.

"That's an interesting point, responded Pinch; and it happens." That leads us to another concept called <u>materiality</u>. Materiality is a nebulous thing that has never been successfully defined, particularly as to quantifying it. Basically, it means that if does not <u>significantly</u> (and usually adversely) affect the financial statements - the heck with it. After all, accounting is not an exact science and the numbers are never penny perfect - except maybe cash. Accounting is more an <u>art</u> than a <u>science</u>. In this case, if the amount is deemed by you to be "material", you <u>modify</u> your opinion.

This brings us to cash. Since cash can easily be proven by a reconciliation process and confirmation with third parties - it is the most "over audited" item in the financial statements. This is particularly true of young and inexperienced auditors.

Other items on the balance sheet can be established by confirming them with third parties. For example, going back to the feed store illustration, you could have written the customer who owed the feed store $1,200 at balance sheet date and said, in effect "Bob's feed store said that on December 31st, you owed them $1,200. Do you admit and agree with them?" If the customer sends it back saying "yup" and signs it - that's purty good proof and support. You could also use this same procedure for the amount that the store <u>owed</u> to the feed mill - the account payable of $1,000.

Other things on the balance sheet can be checked out by examining documents, applying theory, and doing mechanical computations. For example, assuming Bob's fee store paid its insurance premium of $5,000 in June and the insurance coverage was for a year starting on July 1st. At December 31st, it had prepaid expenses (insurance) of $2,500.

Assuming Bob, still owed on his building and he made a mortgage payment of $1,500 on January 5th which was due on December 31st. This payment was $300 principal and $1,200 interest. his balance sheet should show accrued interest of $1,200 - right?

"Aw yeah - I'm kind of getting the hang of things, spoke up Tony, heck, it ain't all that complicated and I can't see what all the fuss is about."

"That's good, replied Lester, but don't get over confident." I have kept this sermon very, very simple and only hit the high spots" the real world is much more complex than Bob's feed store. Trust me.

So far, I have only dealt with a part of balance sheet, and then only with what had been recorded. The tough part of the audit of the balance sheet is dealing with what has not been recorded and with the disclosure (footnote) information.

"You mean to tell me that companies fail to record things?" Asked Professor.

"You bet your fanny" said Pinch. And these things are almost always very bad things. A big part of them fall into a category called contingencies and they are usually almost impossible to quantify.

"Give us an example" asked Cletus.

"The classic item is pending litigation" answered Pinch. Suppose you were Phillip Morris, Inc. and rumors were rampant that a very large Philadelphia law firm was getting ready to file a multibillion dollar class action law suit against you." Don't you think that would present a problem?

"Sure in heck would" answered Tony, but how are you going to figure out what to do about it?"

"You ask questions, said Pinch, and listen very carefully to the answers." You require management to make a formal representation to you and you further require a formal representation from the company's lawyers." Then you see how the company deals with it and if you don't agree with them - you final decision is whether or not to modify your opinion or perhaps even disclaim an opinion." This is called "pucker time".

Now, let's talk a little about the audit of the period of time statement - the statement of operations (profit and loss statement, etc.). The auditor can't economically check out these numbers using the techniques described in the balance sheet audit. The reason being that these numbers are <u>cumulative</u> numbers representing jillions of transactions. it would take an inordinate amount of time to check out all these transaction. Therefore, the auditor, must rely on <u>tests</u> and other things to become "satisfied" with the profit and loss statement.

"How do you know what to test and how much to test" queried Cletus. Is it guesswork?

The golden answer to that question used to be "ICQ and 10%" answered Pinch. To some extent, it still is.

The process is somewhat as follows-

(1) The auditor must become familiar with the company's accounting procedures and determine they are adequate to record all the transactions.

(2) The auditor must become familiar with the company's system of checks and balances - called internal control which, in theory, would assure the proper recording of transaction, the detection of mistakes and fraud. This is by no means fool proof by it is a lot better than nothing.

(3) The auditor should do an analytical review of the operating accounts for the purpose of flushing out abnormal or unusual items and/or trends.

He then develops a plan to test transactions with an emphasis on unusual items and weakness areas of internal control.

Here again - we are dealing with art. Some auditors have developed scientific testing methods based upon mathematic principles and formulas but a good lawyer would make moneys out of them in a court room if they used this stuff as a defense.

I almost forgot another important point about audits. That point is the fact that the auditor must <u>document</u> his work in what are called audit work papers and these work papers must support (prove) his opinion. In litigation, the lawyers have a field day reviewing these documents. (Why do you think the Enron auditors wanted to get rid of them).

There used to be a saying somewhat as follows - a lawyers mistakes are safely locked up behind bars; a doctors mistakes are buried in boot hill; but an auditors mistakes are boldly recorded on parchment for the whole would to see, second guess, and criticize."

My conclusion is akin to the saying about the train - so long as the train stays safely on the tracks and reaches its destination - who cares how it got there; but let it jump the tracks and there's heck to pay. In other words as long as the audited company stays healthy and out of trouble - the auditor is relatively safe regardless of the quality of his audit work papers. But let it "jump the tracks" and there has never been nor will there ever be a perfect set of work papers which will offer the auditor absolute protection from the litigators who go after all the "deep pockets" they can think of. You just do the best you can do and keep plenty of insurance in force. And finally, you very carefully screen all new audit business and stay out of the "bear traps" to the best of your ability. "In other words - don't do any audits for a crook is what you are saying" asked Bulldog. Pinch responded "Absolutely".

"You haven't talked about the auditing rules yet - the gasoline rules I think you called them" observed Tony. "No Tony - said Pinch - not gasoline, just GAAS."

Well, since you all aren't auditors I avoided getting into those details. Basically they require the auditor to do most of the things I've discussed in addition to the following:

1. Plan the audit
2. Be sure you understand the business.
3. Be sure the people doing the work are properly trained and supervised.
4. Be sure everyone involved is independent.
5. Document all the above.

"What do you mean by being independent?" Asked Geek. I don't know anybody who is completely independent anymore. Take Ace sitting over there. They say he is <u>independently</u> wealthy.   He told me most of his wealth was in the form of TXU stock, how independent would you be if TXU went belly up?

"I'd be up crap creek without a paddle" responded Ace.

The accounting profession is very proud of this concept of "Independence". It dates back to the days of the "great depression and stock market crash - 1926" and the logic goes something like this "If the auditor had <u>any</u> financial interest in his audit client it might sway his judgment" (that is, it could raise his materiality level." The though being, if the audited financial statements reflected a false and inflated profit - the stock value would rise and the auditor would have a financial gain. In applying this rule, the pregnancy test is applied. You can't be a "little bit" pregnant - you either are or you aren't. In my mind, the independence rule as it is administered is a slap in the face to the profession. It says - we believe you are a bunch of crooks who would manipulate the numbers to line your own pockets if given the chance. That's pure "bull crap." Independence is a "state of mind" - same as honesty and integrity. You either have it or you don't. There are some interesting things to note while I'm on this subject.

First, the Europeans (especially the British) have no such rule. They believe that the auditor would be more motivated, especially in looking out for theft, defalcations, mismanagement, etc. if he had a financial interest in the client.

Second, the very large firms for years have relied heavily on the very substantial non-audit fees they collected from their audit client – were they truly independent?

You see, the accounting profession is "big business" and operates under the same golden rule. "Them with the gold makes (and enforces) the rules."

"You sound bitter Pinch, observed Tony?"

"How did the profession reach its present state of affairs?" Inquired Professor.

The same way that everything else got to where we are now – it just happened. It is the result of our form of government. The weaknesses and strengths of mankind, changing technology, changing economics, God, the atom bomb, and moral decay.

The accounting profession is the youngest of the professions. It has developed since the stock market crash of 1929 and most of the present rules, etc. have been developed since World War II. I have been a practicing CPA since 1955 and have suffered through many of the changes. In this sermon I am talking from memory and from my soul and expressing only my thoughts and opinions and not trying to present a documented history. What I want to teach is that wiser men than I have helped mold the profession and they have done far more good than harm. However, I feel there could be improvements.

Back in the early days of my career most of the accounting rules we followed were in the Finney & Miller textbooks. The only formal document was ARB 63 which basically addressed a couple of issues which arose in WWII. There was some closed door shuffling going on and emerging was the Accounting Standards Board which began cranking out "cookbook" accounting. The rules (GAAP rules) proliferated and most of them were receiving a push from government, especially the SEC. Each new rule got an "Airing" before it was carved in stone – but do you think they paid any attention to Joe Hayseed, C.P.A., Bowie Texas – heck no. Were they swayed by the Arthurs (Young and Anderson) and the SEC? Does a one legged duck swim in a circle?

And you know what, even with all these wonderful rules – the crap hit the fan again in the late 50's and 60's with some major "audits failures" (train jumping the tracks). And the auditors became the fall guys. And the politicians decided it was high time to do something about it. A couple of fellers named Moss and Metcalf were really stirring things up in Washington and darn near succeeded in regulations the profession. Matter of fact - they won - it is now in effect regulated.

"This is juicy stuff – almost like a soap opera, commented Tony, then what happened?

"Well, the accountants saw the writing on the wall and got busy with some ideas to self regulate and get the heat off themselves". They came up with a new body of rule makers called the Financial Accounting Standards Board (FASB). This board contained some non-accountants and it immediately got busy writing its own "cookbook" and Congress backed off. Also, the auditors commenced to audit the auditors with a process called "peer review.

But the rule making process remained basically the same. A new emergency arose and a new rule was written. It was almost a cat and mouse game. The financial statements preparers were under increasing pressure to show greater bottom line results (profit) and spent hours dreaming up ways of doing this with a pencil.

You've heard the expression "Figures don't lie, but liars figure" I am sure.

"Hold on again" said Tony, you are talking too fast and have switched to Chinese again. How in heck can you create a profit with a pencil is what I want to know?"

A simple illustration would be to move a number – this is called classification or reclassification. Suppose #1 million was moved from salaries and wages (an expense) to goodwill (an asset). This would increase profit by $1 million wouldn't it?"

"Oh yeah, answered Tony, I see what you are saying."

Let me digress for a moment and point out some of the things that were happening in the world – the United States in particular, while the accounting profession was "growing up".

(1) The population was growing older. The average age kept increasing.

(2) Manufacturing was moving from the U.S. to the third world.

(3) Technology was advancing at a breathtaking pace.

(4) The federal government was growing –almost at the pace of technology.

(5) Moral decay was getting worse by the day.

(6) Individual investors were leaving the stock market in droves – those remaining were generally

investing in mutual funds instead of common stocks.

(7) Litigators were having a field day – particularly with class action lawsuits. It is no wonder that

the accounting profession was trying desperately to cover every contingency with a rule.

However, in my opinion, two major mistakes were made in the process. And these mistakes will haunt us for generations.

First, there was an attempt in the early days of the FASB to clearly define the basic concepts (postulates) of accounting. This project was soon abandoned because of its complexity and the major differences of opinion its created. In other words, accountants could not even agree or what an asset is. Can you imagine?

Visualize, if you will, how much simpler accounting, reporting, and audit would be if we had an accounting Bible and a Supreme Court for accountants whose interpretations would be binding to all, including litigators, and will would render formal post release decisions.

The next mistake, I'm my opinion, occurred when the FASB attempted the segregate the rules it was formulating between those which applied only to the large public companies (called big "GAAP") and those which did not (called "little GAAP"). Another failure brought about by disagreement. Today, Bob's feed store must follow the same rules as General Electric. Does this make any sense to you?

Let me make a couple of further points by way of questions.

(1) Do you believe we can eliminate sin by making rules forbidding it?

(2) Do you believe that the federal government can do a better job of regulating the accounting profession that the accountants themselves?

(3) Do you believe that greed, unethical behavior, and immoral acts can be legislated away?

(4) What body today contains 238 convicted felons? (answer U.S. congress).

(5) Do you know of any place on the planet earth more corrupt than Washington D.C.?

"All right Pinch, spoke up Tony, you made your point." Now, how about telling us how all this protects investors."

"Thanks for getting me back on track Tony. The answer is = it does not and cannot protect investors." Remember what I told you in the beginning – financial statements reflect history. Does mankind learn from history? Not all the time!

To be absolutely protected the investor needs to see the future – and that is <u>not possible</u>. So let's look at a few alternatives.

First, let's expand the annual report requirements somewhat. We should analyze the registration statement (initial filing requirements) and see what things included therein might need to be updated on an annual basis.

Next, we should require management to "sign off" on the reports.*

Perhaps the annual report should contain a condensed report and score cared signed off by the stock analyst. For example, he could cover such things as –

(a) Quality of management
(b) Competition
(c) Quality of products/services

*This was done after I wrote this draft – Sarbanes – Oxley act.

And finally, the company's lawyers should be required to include a report (signed of course) covering the company's <u>legal</u> health and current situation.

It's getting late so let me conclude this lecture with a summary. I hope all of you have a better understanding of the complexity of the subject and the fact that I have barely scratched the surface today.

In summary, there will always be risk in investing. Investing decision cannot and should not be based solely on financial statements and auditing opinions (historical stuff). You can't legislate away greed, dishonesty, graft, immoral behavior, unethical behavior, etc. and finally, the government is not the answer to all your problems .... In many cases – <u>it</u> <u>is</u> the problem.

Finally, when someone purchased a stock they should be required to sign a form which says:

1. I read the audited financial statement prior to buying this stock and

2. I relied upon the audit report ___100% ____75% ___50% _____ 0%____ Other _____ in making my investment designs, and/or

3. I relied on the following in making my decision to buy the stock –

   ___Brokers advice   _____ Other (Describe)

   ___Friends advice

   Signed _____ Date _____

Pinch concluded - "The sad thing is, the younger CPA's (under 50) truly believe that accounting is a science and the numbers are precise". Ace asked "Why do you say that - I thought so myself" Pinch responded "I can best illustrate the point with an example."

A young CPA was flying to Los Angeles. He had the window seat and seated next to him was a distinguished looking elderly gentleman. They began chatting and the elderly gentleman said he was a retired brain surgeon.

The young CPA, after introducing himself as a CPA with a very large firm was doing his best to impress the old doctor.

As the plane was flying over the Grand Canyon the CPA looked out the window, saw it, and pointed it out to the doctor who leaned over and peeked out the window to look at that wonder of nature. The CPA asked "do you know how old that is?" The doctor responded "No - do you?" (which was the answer the CPA had hoped for).

The CPA puffed out his chest and said "It is 1 million years 6 days, (and looking at his watch) 16 minutes old." "Amazing, said the doctor, "how did you know that?"

The CPA said it is September 10th - right? Its 11:20 am. - right? The doctor agreed and the CPA beamed and explained.

Last year I was on this same flight - it was on September 4th and I looked at my watch and it was 11:04. The gentleman (who was a geologist with Exxon) who was seated next to me pointed out the Grand Canyon and told me it was a million years old. Simple?

Conclusion - they can be very precise but often not so accurate.

CHAPTER 22

THE AFTERMATH OF ENRON

The good guys on white horses rode in to save us after Enron and the other "cooked books" scandals. Congress, in its infinite wisdom passed the Sarbanes - Oxley act. This act created another government Bureaucracy to audit the auditors. It's called the Public Company Accounting Oversight Board.

And, my fellow Americans, this is only going to cost you $68 million per year - but the good news is, it will put about 300 unemployed folks on the govt. tit and rent 8 vacant office buildings around the U.S. Plus, they can fine them crooked accounting firms up to $15 million. "Ain't that a sweet deal? "Exploded Pinch.

"Horse apples" said Abe. "If there is anything that needs auditing and oversight - it's the Federal Government. There ain't no larger body of cheats, thieves, and crooks on this planet earth than our congress."

"Could that be done?" Inquired Professor. "Bet your hind end it could" answered Pinch. Just turn the "Big 5" (or "3" - or whatever) accounting firms loose and they could audit the heck out of our government - and probably would be delighted to do so. I'm sure their reports would curl your hair."

Pinch added "It would be the first time in our history that the U.S. citizens would get the facts about our actual financial condition. In addition, the auditors should produce another report describing their recommendations for much needed changes.

"Man, that is a great idea" said Professor. "I'll even pay my share of the cost - out of my pocket."

"Me too" said Geek.

"And while the audit is going on - another group of honest lawyers should review all the laws on the books and prepare a report showing -

1. Laws which should be cancelled, and

2. Changes needed to remaining laws" spoke up Abe.

CHAPTER 23

"THE AGE OF ELECTRONICS"

The group had gathered for the regular session and was sitting around, drinking coffee and eating fresh homemade donuts that Julie had sent with husband Bulldog. The usual conversations about the weather and local gossip had started to taper off when Tony announced.

"I was in Fort Worth last week and bought a brand spanking new computer with all the extras (printer, screen, speakers, mouse, etc.) for $649." Also bought a book on how to use it for $19. Now, I'm all set to enter the new era of electronic miracles. My granddaughter got it all hooked up and got me hooked up on the internet too. At her suggestion I went back and bought an Iphone.

What internet service are you using? Asked Professor. American something or other, answered Tony, costs another $29 a month best I can remember." "Aw crap, you should have asked me before you wasted your money, spoke up Geek. "You are getting ripped off by AOL - America On Line." There's lots of other services out there for around $10 a month - just as good."

"What are you going to use the computer for - and do you know how to use it? Asked Professor.

"Well no - but I figure I can read the book and learn how to use it", answered Tony. If my granddaughter, who is 10 years old, can learn to use one of them things, why can't I?

"Cause you're an old dog" said Pinch, and you know what they say - "you can't teach an old dog new tricks." Operating them computers takes a powerful lot of memory work and you ain't got enough memory left to cut it. Besides, what the heck you gonna use that computer for anyway?

Well, I thought I might start writing a book, and put my cattle inventory on it, and keep a budget and a set of books on it, and communicate with my friends, and get educated on the internet answered Tony.

Heck fire, you could have stopped at the dime store and post office and got all the stuff you needed to do that for less than $10 said Pinch. Besides, you ain't about to write no darn book - do you know how tough it is to write a book - shucks - you're talking about a lot of work there and I don't think you would get past Chapter One. What kind of a book you plan on writing?

"I'm not going to discuss it with a pessimistic Professor like you" answered Tony. I'll just do it and if you are still interested. I'll sell you a copy of the book." What are your thoughts about computers <u>Pinch</u>? You use them all the time in your work don't you?

Yep, we started using computers when they first came out - back in the 50's or there about. Computers are a wonderful tool but you have to understand that is all they are - tools. In effect, they are electronic idiots. They only do what they are told to do by their programs.

In the early days they were built with vacuum tubes and mechanical devices and were called "unit" records. They were large, bulky, slow, noisy, and stayed broken down all the time. The programs were an boards, which were wired with little ole short wires - it looked like spaghetti. It was just an electrical circuit. This (and the vacuum tubes) was replaced by a micro chip which a feller at TI (Texas Instruments) invented - and computers started getting smaller - and faster.

Technology kept advancing at a very rapid rate and it seem like a newer and better computer hit the market every week. The programs were now written in a "computer language" and sold in tape or disc form. Basically, everything that anyone conceived that could be done mathematically or electronically (by computers) ended up as a program. Lots of folks were getting rich by figuring out new applications, writing programs, etc. The <u>capacity</u> of the computers was sorely tested and the computer gurus were constantly figuring out new ways to increase the capacity. A whole new language was being developed (i.e. gigabytes).

You were afraid to buy a computer in those days - not only were they being constantly improved, the price kept coming down. I remember that I was financial Vice President for a company about that time and we bought a "computer system" from IBM for about $200,000 as I recall. Within a year we could have replaced it with a couple of "personal" computers costing less than $5,000. And today, the small laptop computers can do much more than anything on the market in those days. So can the Iphones.

"Damnation Tony, you're just like old Etney Burroughs - ask you for the time and you try to tell us how to build a watch. Think the question was "What do you think of computers" said Abe jokingly.

I told you that I thought they are wonderful <u>tools</u> but I foresee trouble ahead because our society has lost sight of that fact and in many cases become almost totally dependent upon them. For example, if you have had any dealing with governmental agencies lately, particularly the IRS - if it ain't on their computer - forget it and now along comes Iphones - where is this going to end. The next generation may be computer literate but completely liberate in other areas - particularly when it comes to using their brain.

Further, we went through a period when the investing public thought there was some sort of magic in computers, the internet, etc. - fortunes were made by a few but lost by many.

The two things that continue to mystify me about people's impressions of computers are:

1. Why is speed so important?

2. What is the true economic substance of the internet?

3. How many years in the future before the internet has any significant positive effect on commerce?

The Professor said "I remember reading a quote once that went something like - if you destroy or eliminate something - be sure you replace it with something of value." It doesn't seem all this electronic gadgetry is doing that".

Abe said "Robert Rourke's quote."

The Professor continued "Steve Jobs died the other day and the news was giving him credit for revolutionizing communications, creating thousands of new jobs, etc, etc." In my opinion, he has destroyed more jobs than he created - along with the devolution of our young people who spend all their time now texting, twittering, etc."

"How did he destroy Jobs?" challenged Geek.

He destroyed publishing Jobs, advertising agencies, other forms of communication jobs" shot back the professor.

"Oh meekly replied Geek.

CHAPTER 24

DRIVERS ED

The gang had started to gather for a mid June session of domino playing and Cowboy busted through the door - red faced and cussin like a sailor. "That darn Abney kid almost caused me to have a wreck - if I could get my hands on him I'd spank his hind end and teach him a lesson".

"Just settle down" advised Abe, "Let's talk about it." "Heck, that kid probably drives better than you anyway." "Like heck he does" returned Cowboy.

Tony stood up and look around the room and announced - "Well gants, it looks like ole Cowboy has introduced the problem for today. I'm sure we can collect our vast experience and knowledge and get this problem solved quickly and get on to something important - like playing dominoes." "For starters, let's make a list of all the bad driver problems we can think of - Professor will you get a tablet and write these down." He sat down as the first hand went up. Abe nodded to Pinch who had raised his hand.

1. Young folks who drive too fast and reckless. Bulldog quickly suggested.
2. Old folks who drive too slow. Cowboy interrupted "Guess that means us middle agers drive just right. Everyone chuckled.
3. Pinch raised his hand and said people who cruise in the left (passing lane) and slow up the smooth   flow of traffic.
4. Tony added. And "rubber necks" who darn near stop to look at every little fender bender.
5. Professor said. I just remembered - people who dart through traffic and pass on the right.
6. Bulldog spoke up and said I have three -
    *People who run stop signs and lights
    *People who turn right at stops without looking - they think they have the right of way.
    *And finally, people who drive without insurance - and I thought of another.
    * Drunk drivers

7. Cowboy said "People talking on the phone while driving".

8. Abe summarized it up by saying.

9. "Drivers today are just D&D. That is dumb and discourteous."

"How do we go about curing these problems" asked Cowboy.

Abe stood and "took the floor" and started his sermon. "First off, there's just too darn many vehicles on the road today and I agree, too many dumber and discourteous drivers. Many of the drivers learn to drive in Drivers Ed classes which don't teach common courteousy and good driving habits, and there aren't enough policemen to enforce the traffic laws. Plus, people with money hire shyster lawyers who get them "off the hook" and they don't pay the price for their traffic law breaking."

Here are some of the things which could be done to cure, or partially cure, some of these problems.

1. Force people to turn in old junkers that can't pass inspection and melt them down as scrap metal.

2. don't allow someone who has received 6 or more traffic citations to <u>buy</u> a vehicle.

3. Use the technology we already have to help control

traffic - i.e.

   *Have radar/camera units in place along highways and at intersections to monitor traffic. Arrest
   violators and allow the <u>film</u> as evidence in traffic court.
   *Use more of the radar/display signs which show drivers their <u>measured</u> rate of speed.
   *Set up "fake" wrecks in school zone to slow down the traffic.

4. Develop a standardized national traffic sign system. I think we need more <u>advance</u> <u>notice</u> signs
   that let drivers know what is coming up ahead of them i.e.

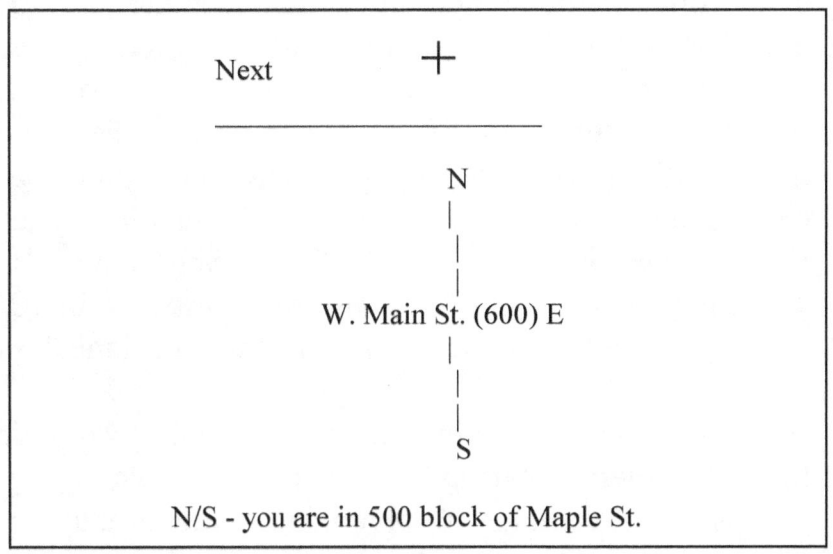

Next   +

N

W. Main St. (600) E

S

N/S - you are in 500 block of Maple St.

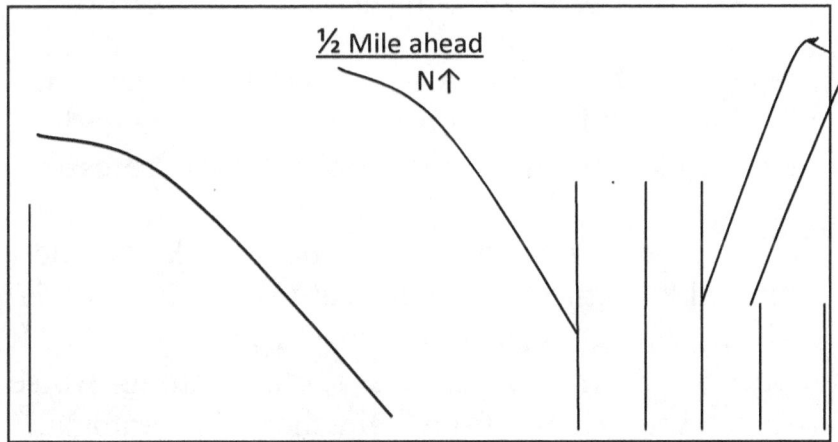

½ Mile ahead
N↑

5. Develop a police vehicle with a fork lift built into the front of it capable of lifting a car and a loud
speaker capable of being heard by drivers with the windows rolled up.

The police officer operating this vehicle would patrol stretches that are chronically clogged up by the slow drivers in the passing lanes. He would pull up behind them and lift their car and as he was moving them over to a right lane he would be explaining over the loud speaker. "You idiot, you were going too slow in the left (passing) lane. If you can't pass and get back into the right lane in 10 seconds or less - stay the heck out of the left lane."

And incidentally, I think the city freeways should have "accident clearing" areas built at least <u>every</u> mile so that vehicles involved in accidents can be moved there quickly and keep the traffic flowing.

"Wal Abe, that all sounds good but it appears to me you just put a bunch on band aids on a huge gash - I don't think that will fix the problem" said Professor.

Tony stood up next and said "Abe, I think you and I think alike - the thing that has to get fixed is the driver - not a bunch more laws, trinkets, etc." "It appears to me that drivers started getting worse when we went from clutches to automatic transmissions and from parents teaching their kids how to drive to turning that responsibility over to Driver Ed schools."

I assume that this is not going to change in the near future so I suggest the following be added to both the curriculum and Driver tests:
   *Driving courtesy

*Dangers in driving
*Dealing with emergencies
*Proper driving habits
  *Passing
  *Entering freeways on the ramps
  *Turning (using signals)
  *Don't tailgate
  *Effects of alcohol on driving

"Well gents, I don't think what we came up with this morning is entirely original - but it's a good start as solving the problem - now we got to get hired by someone or get a government grant in order to get the ball rolling.   Meanwhile, let's play some dominos" concluded Abe.

CHAPTER 25

WHAT ARE WE GOING TO DO
ABOUT THE WETBACKS?

The boys had gathered for their regular meeting, made a big pot of coffee, and started playing dominoes when Ace exclaiming "Where is Cowboy? No one knew so Abe said "I'll call his house - maybe he is sick?" He got up and made the phone call and returned to the domino game and said "His wife said he had to go to Dallas and get a lawyer." They looked at each other and began to speculate as to why Cowboy would need a lawyer - no one came up with a good reason. The door opened and in stepped Cowboy - he got a cup of coffee and sat down. All eyes were on him and he finally said "Them darn DEA fellers came by the ranch early this morning and picked up Jose - my ranch foreman. I went to Dallas and hired a high powered lawyer to try to get him back - it cost me a big wad of money but that slick talking lawyer said he was purty sure he could have him back at my ranch by Tuesday." Is that possible Abe? Asked Geek.

Abe said "Remember us talking about the Golden Rule - with Gold - purt near anything is possible".

Bulldog asked "What is the answer to the wetback problem?" You can't find anyone anymore to do certain jobs; particularly if they involve hard work. And the Mexicans are glad to get the work and do a good job."

Cowboy added "That's true, it took me three years and I don't know how many dead beats before I found Jose. I couldn't do without him anymore. What do you think Abe?"

Abe thought for a minute then said "I think the best solution would be an economic solution - as opposed to a political or other kind of solution. Let me map out what I'm thinking and if Professor would take notes maybe we can get our heads together and fine tune it."

First we need to identify these workers and their dependants. Instead of a green card and social security card we should come up with a special identification card. It should be in both English and Spanish and contain both their picture and thumb print and a unique number - maybe 7 digits.

Second - we must come up with a separate tax structure for them. The tax they would pay would depend upon their classification.

Third - their classification would depend upon the services provided which they would <u>elect</u> and other factors.

"I think you are making this too complicated" injected Professor. "Why don't you shut up" and let him finish" spoke Cowboy in an angry tone. "Ok" said Professor "you don't have to get mad about it." Cowboy just starred him down.

Abe continued "I am trying to keep this simple and avoid another government beau racy. Where was I?"

"Classification" said Geek.

"Thanks Geek" said Abe. "Here is the information we would need for the classifications.

1. Full name
2. Date and place of birth
3. Height, weight, and age
4. Sex
5. Marital status
6. Number of dependents and description

<u>Name</u>   <u>Sex</u>   <u>Birthdate</u>   <u>Speak English</u>

    7. Do you speak English?   Y___   N___
    8. Passed drivers test?   Y___   N___

And here are the options they would have:

    1. Do you intend to enroll your children in
       public schools?   Y___   N___
    2. Do you intend to drive on U.S. roads?
       Y___   N___
    3. Do you have insurance?
       a. Auto liability Y___   N___
       b. Health Y___   N___

    4. Will you use public hospitals? Y___   N___
    5. Have all been vaccinated Y___   N___

From this information a tax structure would be devised somewhat as follows:

Immigrate Tax Structure

Flat tax rates (against wages) to be deducted from earnings:

Base tax - 10%
Tax on dependents - 1% per dependent
Drivers tax - 2%
School tax - .5% per child
Medical tax - 5%
Speak, read, and write English - 3% credit

Now, let's illustrate:

Jose, a 30 year old married male, in good health, married with two school age children comes to U.S. to work on a ranch. His children will attend public schools and family will use public hospitals. He drives but does not own a vehicle. His tax rate would be:

```
*Base tax              10%
*Dependents             3%
*Driver                 2%
*School                 1%
*Medical                5%
       Total           21%
  Credit - English     (3%)
         Net            18%
```

Therefore, his employer must deduct 18% tax from everything he earns. It is that simple.

The Professor spoke up "I agree that the concept is simple, but when you get down to the details it will get much more complex."

"Please give me an example" said Abe.

"The one that came to my mind immediately," answered Professor" is - who gets the tax revenue?

Pinch jumped in "To keep it simple I would suggest the money go to the Federal Government who must remit half of it to the state".

Abe said "That should work".

What about security? Asked Ace. The Geek said "That's easy - add a micro chip to the I.D. card."

Pinch said "Abe, you might be on track for a logical and workable solution to the problem - unless the Politian's screw it up."

CHAPTER 26

PUBLIC EDUCATION

"Boys, let's give the floor to Professor this morning and let him do the talking - he hardly ever gets a word in edgewise" said Abe. Everyone clapped and said "Here" "Here" Professor blushed but finally said "What do you want me to discuss?" "Wal, since you spent most of your life getting educated and then educating others - why don't you just talk about education" suggested Pinch.

"Ok" said Professor. "Since I did not come here prepared to make a speech I'll probably ramble and stumble around so if I get off track please feel free to interrupt me or ask questions at any time." I'm going to try to cover the subject in the following general areas:

  *Purpose of education
  *The need to simplify

*The myth of advanced education
*Moral decay and family life
*The crushing overhead of testing, paperwork, and unrealistic expectations
*Developing the whole child

The basic purpose of education is to train the mind - especially training it to think.

Public education, especially, should be simplified - concentrate on the three R's - reading, writing, and arithmetic.

Advance education has been over stressed. Not everyone needs a PHD.

There has been an ongoing moral decay in our nation and family life has also decayed. Unfortunately, the education system is expected to fill the voids.

Expectations for Public Education have continued to rise and costs have gone up accordingly. The system is expected to develop the whole child.

The educators know "How" to do all that is expected of them - the limiting factor as usual is money - or lack thereof.

Here are a few ideas I have developed over the years that I believe would improve public education.

1. Everything must be in English - period. If the beginning students do not speak English, it should be up to their parents to have them learn English <u>before</u> they enter first grade. This alone would save millions.

2. There should be a more rigid system of screening teachers and of measuring their worth. Those proven to be incompetent should be fired.

3. Schools <u>must</u> keep the student/teacher ratio to 20 to 1 or less.

4. Students should not be allowed to bring cell phones (Iphones, etc.) to school.

5. Curriculum should be developed and taught for subjects necessary to learn for a better life (filling the void described above) - i.e.

*Sex education   *Health
*Effect of Drugs   *Morals
*Voting

That folks, is my top of the head thoughts about Public Education as it exists in the USA today.

CHAPTER 27

POOR CITY DWELLERS

"I'd rather take a beating than drive down to Dallas anymore" said Pinch. "Has anyone been down to that rat race in the Dallas concrete jungle recently". "Yep" said Bulldog. "I can't argue with you - it's a mess down there". "Not just Dallas chimed in Cowboy, I've got an old Buddy named Bud "Knee Jerk" Kotel who drives a big 18 wheeler for Swift. He goes all over the country and he said Dallas is no different from Chicago, Los Angeles or any other city in the U.S.A." "Heaven help us" pleaded Ace.

"Why have things gotten so bad in the cities?" asked Geek. Things are about the same as they have always been out here in the sticks - why don't folks move back to the country if things are so bad in cities?" He added.

"The answer to your second question is rather simple - but the answer to your first question is extremely complex" spoke up Professor. The reason folks don't leave the cities and return to the country or small town is economics. There are jillions of city folk who would move to the country in a heartbeat - except for one thing. There ain't no jobs out in the country and they would starve to death. Just look around here and see how many folks have to commute many miles each day to their jobs - most of which are in the cities or proximity to the cities. I was talking to a feller over in Saint Jo the other day and he said there were eight men who commuted every day to the Boeing Plant between Dallas and Denton. Heck, that is a daily round trip of 150 miles. Those men spend about 3 hours every day just riding to and from work in an old beat up van they bought.

If you look closer at the folks around here, most are (a) retired or (b) wealthy - at least wealthy enough they don't have to work. It's very near impossible to earn a living from the land anymore - unless you inherited one heck of a lot of land like old Cowboy did. Course there's a few who own businesses in the small towns that Wal-mart has not run out of business and a few more who clerk for them. A few others have government jobs and a few get by on welfare. Real jobs are scarce as hen's teeth.

"Yeah, I can see all that" said Professor. If my wife didn't teach school, we would have to pack up and move to the city I guess. She would kind of like to do that anyway I think. She argues with me every time the subject comes up. but, that's beside the point, I'm curious to hear your explanation as to why the cities (especially Dallas) have gotten so bad.

Well, the simple reason again would be "Economics." But that is the "copout" answer. Let's delve much deeper into the subject. First, the problem(s) arise because there are simply <u>too</u> <u>darn</u> <u>many</u> <u>people</u> packed into a relatively small area. (A citizen of China, Japan, or India would laugh at that statement).

Let's look at the things that are affected by the massive input of people into a small area. We'll start with the basic human needs for survival - food, water, shelter, and clothing plus I'll add - jobs, transportation, health care, communication, education, entertainment, getting along within an organization structure, and sex.

The starting point in our analysis is the so called structure. These are the basic things necessary for human habitation and include streets, water, (storage and distribution), sewer, electricity, natural gas distribution, and telephone lines. It is easy to see that any one of these things has its limits. It was designed to handle only so much. If you take it beyond its limits - it breaks. So you see - this is really the old chicken/egg question for the decision makers. Do you project (guess) a large population increase <u>before</u> you build components of the infrastructure or do you <u>wait</u> until the <u>increase</u> has occurred and play catch up? And, who is going to pay for all this good stuff?

We'll discuss the infrastructure in later explanations. Now, let's get back to basics:

(1) Food - Up to now, this has not presented a particular problem. The supply of food is taken care of by competition in our capitalistic society. In reality,

there is an overall surplus of food and much food is wasted in our society. Too much is also consumed I suppose. Just look at all the lard butts out there. As an aside, more of those city dwellers eat out and if you go to any (and I mean any) restaurant in Dallas for dinner - just be prepared to wait an hour or two before you find a place to sit down and eat.

(2) Water - This has already become a seasonal problem despite the fact that Dallas has captured about all the water holes within a hundred mile radius of the court house. During prolonged periods of drought they semi ration the water. They set rules on water usage (such as watering lawns) and switch those that break the rules. I read in the paper the other day that Dallas was sneaking around and buying up land up in Titus county and was going to dam up a creek and create another

"water hole." But the locals (where the lake was to be built) had found out about it and were raising ole Billy goat heck about it." "Horray for them" shouted Geek. "Don't blame Uma darn bit."

"Well, I just had a deep lake built on my place last summer. It probably contains a half million gallons of water. The feller who owned the bulldozers and built the lake (dam) said "before your kids die, they will be able to sell this water to Dallas for about 25¢ a gallon - or maybe more." Said Ace. "I doubt that stated Professor," by then they will be converting the sea water in the Gulf of Mexico to fresh water and pumping it to Dallas."

(3) Shelter – here again – no particular problem. This is another one which gets solved by the capitalistic system most of the newcomers move into rental property

– usually apartments and Dallas got overbuilt on rental property back in the 70's and 80's.

An interest thing I observed in Dallas is that most of the new houses are built in development which are set up as "Homeowner Associations". The theory behind these Associations is to control the quality and aesthetics of the houses and so called common areas so that the property holds its value. Of course, this costs money and the property owners must cough it up in the form of dues they pay to the Association. These Associations are usually managed by a Professional Management Company. Some of them also have "controlled access" (i.e. – fenced, gates, security guards, etc.).

(4) Clothing – no problem – same as food and shelter. The problem is the type of clothing the city folks wear – especially the kids. The boys wear baggy pants that look

like a six year old kid wearing an eight year old brother's hand me downs. And the girls wear blue jeans that look like someone cut about six inches off the topes of them. And of course, they all wear tennis shoes today. You never see anyone in cowboy boots – or even leather shoes.

(5) Jobs – there's a problem here and I think it is much greater than anyone cares to admit. The problem is not just in Dallas – it is throughout the U.S.A. We don't do much manufacturing anymore. We've let all of it escape to the third world countries that have "cheap labor". We depend more on providing "service". I'm here to tell you folks, this is a bad mistake. It will pull the third world up and pull us down – just wait and see.

(6) Transportation – now were getting into some of the visible problems. This is the one which we all see and

which started this conversation. The basic problem is "there" are simply too many cars operating on the present street system." And I'm not sure that simply building more and wider streets will solve the problem.

Some of the Dallas leaders think their new mass transportation system (called Dart "Dallas Area Rapid Transit") will cure the problem(s). I don't think so! The reason is, the traffic patterns in Dallas just aren't that standard – they are more "Helter Skelter." Further, the folks are just too independent and like their driving freedom too much – they ain't going to change unless they have to. The door folks using Dart are the same ones who used to ride the city busses.

In addition, all those cars are creating a heck of a pollution problem.

CHAPTER 28

IS THERE AN EPISCOPALIAN IN THE CROWD?

Most of the protestants religion sects were represented by the group of domino players and there was a sort of unwritten rule that discussion about religion would be avoided. Particularly anything that might be argumentative (and what religious discussion wasn't?)

But, in a small rural community – everyone knew everyone else's business – and religious leanings. Therefore, they all knew that when Bulldog married his present wife Gayle, (both had been married before – him twice and her once). She insisted they join the Episcopal Church (which was in Bowie). She would not marry ole Bulldog until he accepted this commitment. Gayle had been a converted Catholic, but she had been raised up as a Presbyterian. However, the Catholics didn't want her no more after her divorce and especially if she was going to marry a Presbyterian and Bulldog had been purty much a backsliding Presbyterian the past several years so moving over to join the Episcopalians (as he called them) wasn't much of a price to pay for a little smack madam. So they joined the Episcopal Church and even got married by an Episcopal priest.

However, Bulldog soon regretted the move. He commenced to see and hear things about the Episcopal Church that didn't set too well with him. First, a woman got up in church one Sunday and read something from the Bible. The feller sitting next to him explained that she was a wealthy widow from Nocona who contributed heavily to the church and was a lay reader. He said, some Episcopal churches back east even had women priest. And he had noticed two young men always came to church together and sat real close to each other – and when they sang – one of them had a real high pitched soprano voice.

So Bulldog was not surprised at the July meeting when ole Abe boomed out "Is there Ery   Episcopalian in the crowd today?" He knew the question was direction at him.

Bulldog stood up and announced – "Not any more by golly – not after yesterday when they made a cardinal out of an out and out Queer.

Abe chuckled and said "As ole Don Meredith once said-different strokes for different folks." By the way, how many religions are there and which one is best?"

Professor said, There must be dozens throughout the world. Let's see how many we can come up with out of this grump. I'll get started with the largest and try to keep them in alphabetical order: (adherents in parentheses):

*Buddhism (about 360 millions)
*Christianity (Catholic, Protestant, and Orthodox) –
        (about 2 billion)
*Chinese, Religion (about 394 millions)
*Hinduism (about 900 million)
*Islam (about 1.3 billion)
*Jehovah's Witness (about 6.5 million)
*Judaism (about 14 million)
*Mormonism (about 12.2 million)
*Sikhism (23 millions)
*Seventh Day Adventists (about 10 million)

And, of course, there is atheism (a non religion) who teaches there is no God or supreme being. (it has about 1.1 billion adherents)"

Geek had his laptop computer with him so he can look up smaller sects. After a while Geek said, add the following to the list:

*Aladura (1 millions)
*Baha's Faith (5.7 billion)
*Cau Dai (6 millions)
*Confucianism (6 million)
*Falov Gong (10 billion)
*Hare Krishna (1 million)
*Jainism (4 million)
*Rastafari (1 million)
*Shinto (4 millions)
*Spiritaulism (11 million)
*Taoism (20 million)
*Wicca (3 million)

"Why do we have religions and which one is best?"

Asked Ace.

"Now that is a dangerous question and we could end in

a big argument if we all tried to anenwent. So please –

don't anyone start an argument." pleaded the Professor

(a lay reader). He continued.........

"Mankind is a frail thing indeed and faces issues of

health, safety, and morality daily. Religion is the

universal tool for explaining things which we do not

understand through the context of the known physical

world.   Although there are countless religions, each different somewhat from the other, they all serve the same purpose – they answer questions which all humans ask:

*Why are we here? What happens when I die? How shall I live my life?

So you see – the best religion depends on who you are and where you are and what you were taught (and religious)?. Understanding the religious beliefs of others (particularly those in other parts of the world) is one of the most important steps which mankind must take in order to someday prosper together in Peace."

"Give me some examples?" demanded Ace.

Ok - if you were Jewish you would probably chose Judaism because it is the religion of the Hebrews going back to about 1300 B.C. It believes in one God – Yahew.

If you were Arabian you would probably chose Islam and if you lived in India you would probably chose Hinduismioc Buddhism.

But I'm not any of those, I'm an American.

Well, your choice just got a little more complicated. You would probably chose Christianity but you have to narrow that down because there are many segments to chose from. First you must choose between Catholicism, Protestant, or Orthodox.   If you chose Protestant you must chose from (among others) the following:

*Roman Catholic Church   *Pentecostal
*Eastern Orthodox   *Presbyterian
*Baptism   *Seventh Day Adventist
*Anglican (Episcopal)   *Church of Christ
*Lutheran   *Mennonite
*Methodist   *Holiness
*Christian (Disciples of Christ)

This is an over simplification – there are many more "branches." You could spend the rest of your life studying the religions of the world and not cover them all.

The important thing is to select one, that fills your needs but recognize it is not the <u>only</u> religion in the world and respect all others. And don't ever get into an argument about religion – It is a no win subject.

CHAPTER 29

HANGING ON TO IT IS TOUGH – BUT

GETTING A HOLT OF IT IS EVEN TOUGHER

"If most decisions are based on money as certain members of this August group seem to believe; and if the Golden Rule is – him with the gold rules – then it seems that getting a holt of the gold and hanging on to it is very important" is the way that Abe started the March meeting. I personally never did accumulate much and if I didn't have a good pension – I would probably still be working or selling pencils on some street corner in Dallas.

Several of you fellers are alleged to be very wealthy. Would you mind sharing your secrets with the rest of us poor folks?"

There was complete silence – so silent you could hear Professor's pocket watch ticking.

"Come on men – don't be bashful – we won't tell." "What about your big ranches – Cowboy – share your knowledge with the group."

"Aw shucks" said Cowboy, "It ain't that complicated in my business." I'm what you call "land poor" and after that "cow poor." And after that "equipment poor." I got a little dab in the bank and some T-bills. That's about it. Almost forgot – also got a sack full of gold coins down in the bank vault and a rent house in Jacksboro."

"Dadgum" exclaimed Ace, "That's a heck of a lot." I've heard you have 4 sections of land and I counted your cows along the road one day were about three hundred and sixty head - and I'm sure you own more than that."

"Yes, answered Cowboy, about twelve hundred head in all."

Ace, the mathematician, was scribbling on a a sheet of paper and stopped and looked up and exclaimed" Jesus Christ <u>Cowboy</u>, just the land and cows comes to over 3 million dollars.

"Never had thought about it that way" answered Cowboy. How did you figure that?"

"Well, answered Ace, four sections of 640 acres per section equals 2,560 acres. Land around here goes for around $1,000 per acre so 2,560 x 1,000 = $2,560,000. And the cattle would bring, on average, at least $750 per head and that comes to $900,000 (1200 x $750).

"It would be a heck of a lot more than that" injected Pinch.

"How could that be" queried Ace.

"Heck, haven't you ever drove by his place." "What do you think them funny looking things are bobbin their heads up and down out in this pastures?" They ain't peckerwoods boys – them is oil pumps." answered Abe.

"But I don't own them oil wells "exclaimed Cowboy, an oil company up in Wichita Falls own them."

"Yes, but you collect a part of what they produce don't you?"

"Just a little part" defended Cowboy. "My wife's brothers and sisters get most of it." I don't even see my part – it goes straight to a trust the lawyer set up for me to provide for Jeff and Julie's college education. Now that I think of it, I believe that land is in another trust – maybe the cows too. I don't pay no attention to stuff like that – leave, it up to my wife and the lawyer, who is a distant cousin of mine who has his office in Fort Worth. Long as I got tobacco and beer money, I'm fine.

Are you comfortable with the way your wealth is arranged and do you feel it is safe?" queried Pinch.

"Why shore" responded Cowboy. "Long as I got 30-30 bullets for my rifle and .357 bullets for my revolver, ain't nobody going to take my land or cows – I guarantee !!" (Note – it was rumored that Cowboy had once shot one man dead and hanged another one who he caught in the act of rustling some of his cows). Rumor only - never proven.

"So much for hanging on to your stuff, how do you get started in ranching and accommodate wealth in the first place" asked Pinch.

"First, you got to inherit a ranch" promptly responded Cowboy. Else marry someone who owns (or inherits) a ranch.

Everyone laughed. Cowboy looked hurt and said "That's the truth, that's how I got started."

When the group met for its late January session the overall mood was doom and gloom. All the news, especially economic news, was bad. The Republicans had been in control long enough to have everything messed up – good and proper. It looked like any day now El Presidente was going to invade Iraq to take everyone's mind off the economy and hopefully to give it a little kick in the pants to get it moving forward again.

As they sat around drinking coffee and complaining, Ace spoke up and said, "A feller works his tail off all his life trying to accumulate a little something – then the government comes along and starts taking it away from you (taxes) and what they don't get turns to poop in the stock market." How in the heck do you hang on to what you got?"

"There is no absolute bullet proof way" responded Pinch. As long as we live in a capitalistic society there will be risk associated with wealth. It is a proven fact, however, that the best way to minimize risk is to <u>diversity</u>. Remember the old saying "Don't put all your eggs in one basket". – That is the basic concept."

"Aw heck, I've heard that all my life – and it may be true – but <u>how</u> many and what kind of baskets and eggs is enough, asked Ace.

You could ask three experts that question and you would get three different answers – and neither of them would be 100% correct answered Pinch.

Well, I've heard you got a purty good chunk of change – enough to burn a wet elephant at least – so I'll ask you "How would you diversify?"

I have always been a believer in owning dirt. Goes back to what my wealthiest uncle told me about real estate when I was just a kid I guess. He told me – get a lot while you are young. And I did. However, I've always tried to keep my wealth invested in the following categories and amounts.

(a) Real estate   60 to 65%

(b) Stocks and bonds
     *Bonds   12 to 15%
     *Stocks   10 to 15%

(c) Oil and gas   4 to 7%

(d) Cash and cash
     *Equivalents   5 to 10%

Bear in mind, I'm talking about preserving wealth – not accumulating wealth. That means in each of the categories above you would try to invest in the safest thing available. In stocks, as an example. You would stick to the solid "blue chips." I've heard some expand say you also ought to keep a tad (maybe 1%) of your wealth in Gold (i.e. Kruger and coins) just in case there was a <u>total</u> collapse in the economy. That don't make a heck of a lot of sense to me – I'd prefer to have a good shotgun and a case or two of shells for that contingency.

I'm always reminded of an expression which my late father in law used a lot "Spanish-translated, the saying is "The one that knows – knows." The wisdom to impart from this ancient saying is simply "turn your investments over to an expert" and trust him to give you good advice and guidance. I'm talking about a major brokerage house such as Merrill Lynch or Morgan Stanley, etc.

CHAPTER 30

SCATTER IT OUT GOOD LORD!

"I'd like to know more about the economy" announced Professor as the grand commenced to gather for the regular session of dominoes, whittling, spittin, & gossip.

"What would you like to know" answered Pinch.

All I read and hear on the news says the economy is recovering and everything is good – yet I seem to be broke all the time and most of my friends are broker than me.   Heck, I stopped and got some gas put in my old pickup this morning and it cost me $3.60 a gallon.   My pension check don't seem to go around anymore – and I ain't run into anyone in person who says the economy is good.   Is there anybody in this room who thinks the economy is good?   Dead silence.   What about you Tony -

you're always bragging on the elephant people – the Republicans. Do you think the economy is good?

"Well, it ain't exactly good but I believe it is improving" responded Tony.

Improving from what? angrily countered Pinch. From the way it was when old "Slick Willie" Clinton was in charge? You're crazier than a Bessy bug if you think that! It seems to me that the national economy is always better when the Democrats are in power than when the Republicans are in power – why is that?

Pinch started to give an educated answer about supply and demand, the monetary system, interest rates, unemployment rates, etc. and it was obvious that he was not getting through to anyone.

Bulldog interrupted him with, "I don't mean to be disrespectful to you but what you are trying to explain to us just confused us more. Heck, we aint economists."

"Well excuse me, retorted Pinch - if you are so darn smart, than perhaps you can explain things better in your more earthy language."

I'll sure try said Bulldog. It puts me in mind of a story my uncle Josh told about Joe Bob Capps when Joe Bob got religion. He went out behind the barn and got down on his knees and was praying "Lord – rain down stones on all the sinners!" Todd, uncle Josh's youngest boy, was in the barn milkin the old Guernsey cow and he overheard Joe Bob shouting louder and louder – "Lord, Lord – rain down stones on all the sinners." He quit milking, slipped outside and filled his pockets with some rocks and went back into the barn and climbed up into the hay loft and worked his way over to the door which was on the second floor (loft view) and almost directly over the kneeling Joe Bob. He positioned himself by the door and listened intently – trying to decipher Joe Bob is mumbling. Drecley, Joe Bob cut loose again with "Oh Lord – rain down stones on all the poor wretched sinners." Todd reached in his pockets and got two handfuls of rocks and dropped them on Joe Bob's head. Joe Bob jumped up and yelled – "Scatter em out good-Lord – scatter em out good."

What in heck does that old bullcrap story (who everybody has heard before) have to do with explaining the difference between a donkey (democrat) economy verses an elephant (republican) economy? Angrily queried Pinch.

"Why heck – that <u>is</u> the difference!" retorted Bulldog.

"I don't get it" said Geek. "Neither do I" said Tony." "Neither does anyone" mumbled Ace.

"Maybe a little explanation is in order" conceded Abe. So listen carefully.

The economy in general (especially the world economy) is extremely complex and few (if any) understand it completely.   There are too many relationship and inter relationships. When you examine the U.S. economy you must also take into account the world's economy.

By far the greatest <u>force</u> is today's U.S. economy is the Federal Government. It redistributes wealth (money) – big time, it is <u>the</u> majority when it comes to spending.

The Republicans are controlled by big business and wealthy folks – always has been, always will be. Both big business and wealthy folks have one thing in common – Greed! Big business wants to show a bigger profit and accumulate more wealth – and wealthy folks just want more wealth.

And once these folks get their hands on the money, they don't spend a heck of a lot of it. The wealthy might build a new castle and put a few carpenters and bricklayers to work – or buy a yacht and go on a cruise. Big business pays off the lobbyist and politicians and gives their executives a fat bonus. But for the most part, the money doesn't get circulated and money movement gets constipated.

The Democrats, on the other hand, scatter it out real good. They create new Bureaucracies and put lots of folks (mostly Democrats who are mostly minorities and pore folks) to work and they spend the heck out of the money. The Democrats also gives a bunch of it away in the form of grants and loan a bunch of it to foreign countries. What they accomplish is to scatter the money out good so it can be spent and money movement stays regular. "Makes sense to me" agreed Geek.

As they were departing, Pinch walked over to Tony's truck and Tony rolled down the window. Pinch said "Tony, I apologize for responding to you so angrily." Tony looked him in the eye and answered "Pinch, I don't want to cause you any harm - but I hope that when you get home your mother jumps out from under the porch and bites you" - then he spun his tires as he left.

CHAPTER 31

TODAY, LET'S TALK ABOUT SOMETHING

INTERRESTING – SEX!

The crowd had assembled and several groups were clustering around the room and were starting to talk about the usual subjects - last night's news, the weather, politics, etc.

Bulldog began rapping his coffee cup with his spoon and when he got everyone's attention, he stood up and said, "Gang, let's talk about something interesting today – like sex."

"I like sex" said Geek. "So do I "echoed Bulldog.

"Yeah, but you guys are young, butted in Pinch, all of us old farts used to like it."

"Speak for yourself" spoke up <u>Tony</u>, "Don't put all of us senior citizens in the same category with yourself."

"I heard ole <u>Abe</u> got a hold of some of them niagra pills" whispered Professor into Pinch ear. Pinch laughed out loud.

Tony said "All in all, sex is for young folks. They say if newlyweds would get a big jar and put a bean in it for every time they had sex, they would fill the jar with beans the first year. Then, starting with the second year, if they removed a bean every time they had sex – it would take them the rest of their lives before they emptied the jar."

"Aw heck, I don't believe that," said Geek.

"Wal, I'll tell you what by gosh, I'll just prove it to you with that group of studs (and past studs)" rebutted <u>Tony</u>. "Let's take a poll."

"That won't work, said Abe, everyone will lie if they have to tell about their sex life."

"No they won't, countered <u>Professor</u> we'll use "secret ballots." He then explained how to conduct the poll". First, he said, there are 6 men here this morning. Let's first find out something about our group – raise your hand for the following – we'll use secret ballots when we get to the nitty gritty" he then got a legal pad and pencil and commenced to ask questions, count hands, and write.

<u>Question</u>

<u>Count</u>

    How many are under 21?

    How many are between 21 and 45?

    How many are over 45?

       Total

This don't tally up said Abe, who didn't vote? Professor raised his hand and said "I don't want to participate in this vulgar mess."

"Mark him down in the over 45 category" laughed Abe.

<u>Abe</u> Continued.

How many are married now?

How many have been divorced?

How many are widowed?

How many have never been married?

"Now let's finish this poll" said Abe. He then passed out little stacks of scraps of paper to each on in the room and asked "Anyone need something to write with". A few raised their hands and he gave them stubby pencils. He said, "From here on, when I ask the question, write down your answer and I'll pass my hat and collect your answers. There should be some interesting results:

Answers   <u>Average</u>

On the average, how many times a week
    are you having sex now?   1 to 4

(<u>Cowboy</u> had asked "Do you mean with
women only?" And everyone laughed.
They laughed again why Bulldog answered
"Yeah, sheep don't count")

As best you remember – answer these –

How many times a week were you having sex
    Five years ago?   1 to 8
    Ten years ago?   3 to 15
    The first year of your first marriage?   10 to 40
    The first year of your <u>last</u> marriage (only those
        married more than once answer this please).   3 to 5
    How many times did you have sex before you
     got married   0 to 3
    Did you ever have sex with your shoes off
     before you got married   2 yes
    Have you had sex with anyone other than
        your wife since you married?   3 yes
     With how many women?   8
     How many times   25
(Pinch thought – ole <u>Abe</u> might have skewed
those last two answers)

"Isn't this fun? asked <u>Geek</u>. "It's a lot more

interesting than the stuff we usually talk about – doesn't

everyone agree?"

Most did.

Pinch observed. "Based on the results you showed us – I'd say the old folks are getting their share of sex.

"Is that really true?" Asked Bulldog. "I had always heard that people quit having sex once they got around 60 years old."

"That may have been true years ago, answered Pinch, "but it ain't true no more."

"What caused the change?" inquired Geek.

"Let me try to answer that one, since I'm the senior senior" said Abe. No one objected so he continued. There are several factors, the most important being:

*Advances in drugs and medicines
*Improved diet and health
*The sexual revolution and
*Improved communication

Let's look at each of these:

Today, science has developed several "miracles" for old men that allows them to get erections. These include the miracle pill – Viagra, another liquid drug injected into the thing (can't remember its name), and doctors can now even implant a pump into a man so he can pump his old thing up anytime he wants to. There are also hormones for old women that keep them perking.

Next, people eat better, exercise, and are healthier than they used to be.

The sexual revolution came along and women folks became more aggressive sexually and more truthful. They admitted that they enjoyed sex as much as men – oftentimes more.

And finally, improved communications allowed old folks looking for a sex partner to hook up. For example, the internet and email, and "getting personal" ads. There are more ads from older women for a stiff tool than from older men looking for some smack madam.

Abe continued "While I was talking it hit me that sex in your older age is more dependent and controlled by the female rather than the male. Therefore, before a young man marries he should spend as much time with his prospective in-laws as he can. He should observe the momma and talk to the papa. Ask about their sex life, etc. look at them carefully. His future bride will act and look a lot like her mama!"

"That gives me something to look forward to in old age" said Geek as the dominoes were shuffled and the games began.

After they broke up and as Abe was getting into his pickup, Professor walked up and asked "Abe, I'd like to find out more about that stuff you were talking about". "Fine, said Abe, jump in your truck and follow me to my house and we'll talk about it." And they did.

CHAPTER 32

WHAT IS THE BEST PROFESSION THESE DAYS?

It was early Spring and the grass was starting to grow and leaves had begun to appear on the trees. The weather was absolutely delightful that morning as the men gathered to start another session – all except Cowboy who was on vacation in Sante Fe, New Mexico. Joe Frankel, his cousin was filling in for him.

After the domino game had started, Abe cleared his throat and asked "Gentlemen, what shall we discuss today? After several subjects had been nominated, it was obvious that none of them had much appeal. Joe Frankel spoke up "Can I make a suggestion? "Sure" said the judge. Joe said, my oldest daughter it graduating from high school in about two months and she keeps asking me "What is the best profession to enter these days? Since I didn't go to college I don't have a good answer for her – can you help me?

He followed up –

"I know that this group contains several successful professional men that my cousin described –

For example – Judge Abe Hardhart – Law

　　– Dr. Antonio Gomez – Medicine

　　– Lester Green – Accounting & Business

　　– Cletus Carpenter – Education

　　– Stuart McGraw – Engineering and space travel

The judge asked "everyone agree on the subject for today?" Yeah, yeah, yeah, yeah.

So the judge said, "I'll get started then and I'll tell you from the start – I darn sure don't recommend law. One of the biggest problems in this country today is – there's too doggone many lawyers – and too many bad laws. Everybody will tell you that our system is the best in the world – and maybe it is. But it sure is far from perfect. Congress passes too dam many laws that just don't make any sense except maybe for the "special interests" that rushed them through. There are far too many "do gooder" laws forced on us. The law makers (congressmen) are cranking out too many "thou shalt" laws instead of "Thou shalt not" laws. They are trying to control our lives.

"What do you mean by that?" Interrupted Tony. The judge said "Tony, you smoke cigarettes and I've never seen you with your seat belt buckled in your pick up." You break the law every 30 minutes or so. "Well" said Tony, "It's a free country isn't it?" "No" said the judge, "far from it." "Matter of fact, it's a doggone expensive country – thanks in great part to laws and lawyers."

There use to be an example that lawyers used to illustrate what I'm trying to get across.

If a town has only one lawyer - he will likely starve to death. But if a second lawyer moves in to the town – both will get rich.

There are so many lawyers today that they have specialized. Just look in the yellow pages. There is a lawyer for about everything you can imagine.

Geek interrupted "Judge, if you were to become a lawyer, what kind would you recommend?"

The wise old judge pondered the question for a minute and finally said "If a person wanted to make a lot of money from lawyer he would become a "damage" litigator, divorce lawyer, or criminal lawyer – and work on a contingent fee basis but only accept cases that had the potential for really "Big bucks".

"How does that work?" Asked Joe Frankel who was visitor today and had suddenly taken a serious interest in what the old judge was saying.

"Well, answered the judge, let me answer that with a hypothetical case.

A school bus is stopped and unloading two students, a big tanker truck crashes into the bus and kills four students and injures six others. A lawyer is hired by the parents to sure the owner of the tanker truck (a big oil company). He takes the case on a contingent fee basis (usual about one third of damages recovered). The case goes to trial and the lawyer gets it set for a trial by jury. Of course, the big oil company (defendant) and his insurance company has hired the best Philadelphia law firm that money can buy to defend it. The trial becomes a three act play and the opposing lawyers are the "directors." Whoever puts on the best show convinces the jury to rule in his favor – and his side wins. During this process – the case may be settled "out of court – and often times is." In this illustration, the oil company has offered $30,000,000 to settle and the plaintiff accept. The lawyer collects $10,000,000 for his fee.

"Golly, said Geek, that sounds like easy money. I don't see why everybody doesn't want to be that kind of lawyer.

The old judge chuckled "It's not as easy as I made it sound. It's a rare thing for a lawyer to get such a case and often times the "Philadelphia" lawyers, win, and the lawyer gets zero.

Well, do you recommend that Joe's daughter studies law? asked Tony.

"Definitely not" answered Abe, and neither do I recommend politics."

Tony, please give us your thoughts on the medical profession.

Anthony Gomez, MD. Said "I'm afraid that what I'm about to tell you about the medical profession is as gloomy as what Abe told you about the legal profession.

When I attended medical school many years ago we learned of the history of medical and of the value of the proper applications of ordinary human feelings and compassion (known as bedside manners). We also studied health science, biomedical research, and medical technology. After I graduated and completed my internship I joined an elderly Doctor named Dr. John

Boitnett in San Antonio and worked with him for 11 years until he passed away. Then I joined the staff at the Santa Rosa hospital in San Antonio and worked there for forty years until I retired.

In the early years of practice I truly loved what I was doing. Patients came to our office and we made house calls. Most of our patients were poor Mexicans and they could not always pay our fees. But they paid what they could and did yard work, house work, etc. for the balance. We were not getting rich but each made a very comfortable living.

During the past 50 years, there have been unbelievable strides in medicine and medical technology. It has been impossible to keep up with everything and the medical profession has become highly specialized.

Geek raised his hand and Tony recognized him with "Yes Geek" Geek asked "What was your specialty Tony?"

Tony answered "None, I suppose – I practiced in the area called "Internal Medicine."

"Did you make a lot of money and are you rich?" blurted out Geek.

Tony paused before answering – "Yes and no Geek – I am rich in memories of the hundreds of beautiful babies I delivered and poor people I healed but I am no multi millionaire by any means. I worked hard and saved my money and invested it wisely and will always be able to live comfortably and not want for anything.

"Heck doc" said Ace, "you ain't said nothing but good about doctoring – what's wrong with it?

Ace, I was getting to the bad stuff before Geek interrupted me. What's wrong with the medical profession today is politicians and lawyers and lawyers and politicians – either way, they have nearly ruined the medical profession.

Let's start with the lawyers. In Abe's "hypothetical lawsuit" illustration he could just as easily used a doctor as the defendant and patient as the plaintiff who believed he (she) was damaged by the doctors treatment. There are so many lawyers today who will take any case involving alleged malpractice (on a contingent fee basis) that the cost of our malpractice insurance has skyrocketed. Doctors and hospitals have added so many protective procedures, etc. that affect treatment that I sometimes wonder if patients and always properly treated.

And politicians have created so many laws and programs that we are on the very edge of pure "socialized medicine" in the U.S.A.

Ace blurted out – "I keep hearing "Socialized medicine on the T.V. and everywhere – what the heck is it anyway and why is it so bad?"

"Well Ace," said Tony, I'll give you a simple explanation because a detailed explanation world require hours of my time and yours.

"Keep it simple Doc so I can understand it." said Ace.

Tony said "Socialized medicine is a system of medical care that is publicly financed, government administered, or both. That means simply that you would be paying for Ole Leroy Lapson's doctor bills and the federal government would control medicine and health care."

"Heck, I can see why that's bad" responded Ace. I'm against it myself" (everyone laughed).

"In closing, said Dr. Gomez, the practice of medicine has gone to the dogs like about everything else in this country and I'm glad I got out when I did. And no, I would not recommend it as a profession today.

"Thanks Doc," said Abe. Let's take a smoke break and then Pinch can talk about accounting. (The smokers went outside and smoked and in about 15 minutes they came back in and sat down).

Pinch commenced talking. "Fellers, if you remember I discussed the auditing side of the accounting profession a couple of months ago – right after the Enron fiasco. Things haven't improved any since then. Matter of fact, they have gotten worse – much worse. It is doubtful in my mind if the accounting profession as I know it will survive.

"Why do you say that?" asked Abe.

Because the profession is dominated by a bunch of weak kneed CPA's and others who live in mortal fear of the federal government and believe that they can be saved from federal regulation by creating all sorts of boards, rules and regulations, etc.

"Isn't that what they need?" asked the Judge.

"You sound like a lawyer/politician now" responded Pinch. "In my opinion," said Lester. "The profession began its downhill plunge about the time this nation began its downhill plunge – right after World War II. It accelerated the fall with the maturity of the baby boomers and the massive moral decay of this nation." Everyone wanted to get rich – regardless of how it was done. This included many (far too many) accountants.

Early in the game, the Financial and Accounting Standards Board (FASB) was a good idea and I thought it would improve the profession – especially when it started its accounting concepts project. Under this project, as I visualized it, an accounting <u>bible</u> would have been created which would have been a very useful <u>tool</u>. The other project which I had great hope for was the "Big GAAP/little GAAP project. The second project never got off the ground. A project that did get finalized was the peer review project. At first I was in favor of that project also but it has evolved into something far different than I envisioned. Had it concentrated on "finished product" rather than rules and procedures - I think it might have worked. But the firms that have since been involved in the accounting scandals had all <u>passed</u> their peer reviews. What does that tell you?

Bulldog blurted out "It tells me that you are talking Chinese - I don't understand what the heck you are talking about.

"I suppose you are right, Bulldog answered Pinch. It is very complex and confusing due primarily to external pressures on the profession these past few years and the muddled solutions to those pressures which I have described today and in prior meeting . Give me a minute to collect my thoughts and I'll try to carry you through this mess in layman's terms."

"Before you start, may I make a suggestion?" Interrupted Tony.

"Sure" answered Pinch.

Ton said "Why don't you tell us what you would do to fix the accounting profession if you were given that opportunity?"

"Great suggestion" said Pinch. Let me think about it for a few minutes before I begin.

"Ok - here goes" said Pinch. The first step would be to divide the certification and licenses into two classes - private and public. It follows then that all the rules, regulations, etc. would likewise be divided along the same lines. The public class could serve public companies as well as private companies. The private class could not provide "attest" (audit) service for public companies. There would be two distinctly different certificates.

Generally Accepted Accounting Principles (GAAP) would be broken down into two segments - (A) fundamental which would be <u>mandatory</u> for <u>all</u> and (B) public company which would only be applicable to public companies.

You ask how I would straighten out the mess we are in? Assuming I had dictatorial powers, this is the way I would do it.

Let's start with the rules for accounting and reporting - those things we now call <u>Generally</u> <u>Accepted</u> <u>Accounting</u> <u>Principles</u> or simply GAAP. (Better yet - call them Dictated Accounting Principles (DAP).

First, I would set up a <u>bible</u> which would contain only the basic concepts which everyone would be required to follow. It would contain such things as:

1. Definitions of assets and liabilities

2. Historical cost concept

3. Matching of revenue and expenses concept

4. Economic substance over form

Second, in loose leaf form I would set up required applications of the concept contained in the bible.

These would apply to the private CPA's as well as the public CPA's.

Next, again in loose leaf form, I would set up special rules and applications which applied only to public companies and CPA's.

Then I would take this same approach to auditing - or GAAS.

Audit bible

Required applications for all public company only.

Next, I would establish a paid staff of "experts" who would provide <u>technical</u> services for a fee to all - public, private CPA's and public CPA's. This body would also be given the task of educating the populace on "How to read and understand financial reports."

And finally, I would establish an <u>appeal</u> process. (Create a board of appeals).

Related to the above, I would also:

1. Require passing a test about every 4 or 5 years in order to renew your license.

2. Redirect the "Peer Review" program to <u>concentrate</u> on results (reports produced) rather than methodology.

"It seems like you want to scrap what we now have and start over" said Ace.

Not exactly, said Pinch "What I want to do is get back to where we were before the profession went stir crazy because of fear of government control.

When I entered this profession we had none of this literature (which I will refer to as crap) but we did just fine. GAAP was basically the Finney & Miller Accounting Textbook and GAAS was the Montgomery Auditing Textbook. As a CPA you applied those concepts and were required to use professional judgment. If you used bad judgment, you got sued and lost your license - it was that simple. This has never been a forgiving profession.

"I'm not understanding some of the things you are explaining, said Bulldog, can you make it simple for me?"

Pinch said, "let's look at it this way."

First, a financial statement reflects financial <u>history</u>. The balance sheet shows financial position at a point in time. The profit and loss statement shows the results of operations for a <u>period</u> of time. There is much judgment involved in preparing them and they are <u>far</u> from "penny perfect."

Most people who read financial statements do not understand this. Sophisticated investors do understand this and do not make their investments decisions based solely on financial statements - audited on otherwise. Most banks do not require audited financial statements any more from borrowers.

And try as we might, we are not legislating away sin. There will always be liars, cheats, etc.

We have stopped using our brains and rely far too heavily on computers, electronics devices, etc. we are becoming stupider by the day. We are devolving. The rule makers are trying to convert <u>art</u> to <u>science</u> - and it is not working. Their current project is trying to force their rules on the entire world. DUH!

Abe said "Pinch, you got a little worked up over accounting - would you recommend it as a profession?"

Pinch said "No, it is a terrible profession as things now stand. However, the question should be would you recommend accounting as college major? And my answer to that question would be yes, if you would like to go into business or become a financial executive - accounting is a great foundation for those jobs. "The language of business is often used to describe accounting."

Abe said "Professor - you are up."

The Professor said "Ace, do you want to change place - Pinch is a hard act to follow?" Ace said "Think not." So the Professor continued.

"The greatest problem in the education field today is money or the lack thereof". Substantially all money for education comes from tax revenue - and when politicians start "cutting" budgets, one of the first things they reduce is budgeted funds for education."

Another major problem is the language barrier - this ties in with the immigration problem.

Another problem is curriculum mix - we do not teach near enough science and math.

And that's about it" Concluded Professor.

Pinch said "You don't seem to think there is anything wrong with the education profession - do you recommend it?"

The Professor counted "in my opinion, there is nothing wrong that can't be fixed with more money. And yes, I recommend it. I must hasten to add - I only recommend it to those who have a "calling" and will recognize they will never become wealthy in the Profession."

Professor looked at Ace and said "your turn."

Ace said "The engineering profession, like everything else, has been adversely affected by the lousy economy these past three years. There is a surplus of engineers today and many, many of them are unemployed."

In the final analysis, engineers design and/or build stuff. So much of this is done today by computers.

However, if the economy ever gets straightened out again and we get back to building stuff - I highly recommend engineering.

Abe said "That wraps up the Professions we outlined at the start of the meeting - does any else want to add anything?"

Joe said "Thank you very much gentlemen - this has been very enlightening - I'll tell my daughter what you said."

Abe, the wise old our stood up and said "Joe, please don't try to influence your daughter's career decision based or what we said today. There are hundreds or even thousands of other careers to choose from. Most schools provide career counselors to assist students select their career. I suggest you use one. I have always envied people who decided early in life what they wanted to do in life - did it - and were happy with their choice. Likewise, I admire folks who are not happy with their choice - and change it later in life. And everyone can't be a doctor, lawyer, accountant, or engineer - matter of fact, a "trade" might be a better choice in today's screwed up world.

CHAPTER 33

TAKING SCALPS

At the next meeting, even before all had gotten their coffee and sat down, Cowboy said "Pinch, I been thinking about what you said a long time ago and I don't agree with you 100%.

Pinch asked "What is it you don't agree with?" Cowboy said "You said everything is based on money, but I don't believe that. For example, they arrested my buddy Joe Bob last summer for rustling and everyone involved lied like dogs to get him convicted and sent to prison - their decision weren't based on dollars." "Ask Abe the Judge."

Abe thought a minute and responded "I think what Cowboy is talking about is this. In law enforcement, government regulation, and some other not for profit operations it is difficult to measure decisions in dollars. Therefore, they have reverted back to the ways of the Indians."

"You really got me confused now Judge" said Cowboy. You got to explain that one for damn sure."

Abe said, "Let me give you a few illustrations." First, take the local Sheriff - he is elected by the citizens and is put on a salary. How is he ever going to get a raise? He doesn't operate for a profit - just the opposite - his department costs the citizens tax money to operate. How can he show the voters he is doing a good job and deserves more money?

Cowboy said "By cutting down on crime," by arresting the criminals."

The Judge said "True - and we call that "Taking Scalps." But it is also true that in the process many scalps are taken from innocent people. This same thing happens in regulatory authorities - they very aggressively pursue <u>any</u> <u>chance</u> at taking a scalp - regardless of the alleged damages.

Cowboy said "Judge, you are making some serious charges against very important people - aren't you afraid of getting sued or something?

The Judge chuckled and said "At my age - who cares what I've just told you has been going on forever and those in the know have always been aware of it."

"Did you allow any of it in your Court room?" Inquired Pinch.

Abe said "Let me tell you boys what a court case (especially one heard by a Jury) is about. It is really similar to a play.

The players are the defendant and the witnesses; the directors are the two lawyers - prosecuting and defense. The Judge is the producer and the jury is the audience. Which of the directors puts on best show - wins. If a Director (Lawyer) gains a reputation of putting on good shows and winning - he earns a lot of money and usually becomes rich.

Cowboy said "Then lawyering must be the best profession to get into."

CHAPTER 34

MINERAL RIGHTS VS. LAND OWNERS

The Professor showed up late for the next meeting. Everyone was speculating as to why. Finally he showed up - mad as an old wet hen.

"What's the trouble?" Inquired Abe. "It's those damn oil companies" responded the Professor. "They think they own this country now - they are all over the place - drilling wells and tearing hell out of the roads. Plus, every time you start down a country road around here you either fall in behind one of their big trucks hauling equipment or a tanker truck hauling oil or salt water and creating a cloud of dust - you can't pass them on these narrow roads. And if you meet them, you had better pull off into a ditch and let them through." And when they are setting up a drilling rig - they block the road for hours. I'm about ready to start carrying a shotgun loaded with buckshot so I can teach them a lesson."

Pinch chimed in "I had a seismic crew try to convince me they had the right to come on my place - I finally called a lawyer who somehow kept them off - and a "Land man" hounded the hell out of me trying to get me to sign a lease."

Ace said "We had a problem with one of them who wanted to lay a pipeline across our property."

Cowboy remained silent during this discussion.

Abe finally said "Texas is one of the states that allows mineral rights to be separated (and owned) from surface rights - and the mineral rights supersede the property rights. That means the mineral rights owner can come on to the property <u>without</u> obtaining permission from the property owner."

"That is not fair nor right" angrily responded Pinch.

"I have been trying to tell you for months - nay years - that many laws are not fair" responded Abe. In this case, the laws are extremely complex and the best advice I can give you is "Hire a good lawyer who is experienced in this area of law if you have a problem." Said Abe.

Cowboy finally said "Abe is right - we have the mineral rights on nearly all of our property but we still hired a good lawyer in Wichita Falls to advise us before we signed a lease. It sounds to me like none of you fellers got the mineral rights when you bought your property - and you ain't got many rights when it comes to oil and gas."

Pinch said "I just might start a campaign to get the damn unfair laws changed."

Abe said "I know you have lots of money Pinch but the odds of you winning are slim to none."

CHAPTER 35

WHAT IS THE KEY TO A HAPPY LIFE?

Cowboy said – "Fellers, we have covered some deep subjects in our past domino sessions. Sometimes when I get home I'm still thinking about what someone said and I might ask my wife's opinion on the subject. All of you who know her knows that she will have her own opinion on every subject. She fusses about our wasting so much times at our domino parlor and that we should stay home some and help around the house. Personally, I think the women folk are just jealous of our set up."

"Amen" Chimed in Ace, then followed with "I was lying in bed last night and couldn't go to sleep. I got to wondering, what is life all about and what is the most important thing or rule you should follow in life?"

"What is the key to a happy life?" Tony said "That's easy – stay healthy and enjoy life. "Naw, that ain't it, it's going to church on Sunday and following the golden rule" spoke up Professor.

"I remember a poem once about leaving fingerprints on the sands of time – that's what I want to do – something important and lasting" said Ace.

In my mind "It's accumulating a lot of wealth" said Pinch "money ain't no good if you ain't healthy "interrupted Professor" and you durned sure can't take it with you – just ask old man Crenshaw." "Who is old man Crenshaw?" asked Geek. "He's dirt now – he was my wife's dad" Ace explained.

"Let's hear what old wise one thinks" spoke up Bulldog. Abe "Tell us who is right?"

Abe said "Each of you are partly correct – but the key is – peace of mind." It would probably take a different recipe for each of us to reach that goal.

The Professor said "I apologize in advance for rambling around but there are several things I want to get off my chest this morning – I saw some pompous know it all flapping his gums on T.V. last night and it just made me mad. Americans can be and usually are so durn stupid." "Does that include us?" Asked Pinch. "Does if you don't agree with me" shot back Professor, then he let rip:

1. Throughout history nations have risen to power – stayed on top a while – then fell off the throne (or more often got knocked off) after a time. We are fooling ourselves if we think different about the

U.S.A. – we are falling as I speak. Most of the world hates us and will cheer when we crash.

2. Politics is really about "borders". For too long we have placed far too much power at the federal government level – to the point that Washington dictates much of our lives and all of our economy."

3. Maybe we need a <u>dictator</u> for a while to straighten out the mess in Washington – I propose that he start by ordering a complete and thorough audit of our government. (And yes it could be done – and needs to be done before we, as a nation, become bankrupt.

4. Things really went from bad in worse a few years back when the lawmakers started producing "thou shalt "Laws instead of "thou shalt not" laws.

5. I think Malthus was right – we are rapidly over populating and starvation will ultimately get us.

6. With so many people unemployed and hungry – before they began to starve, there are going to be some grand revolts. If you are among the rich, you had better build a large moat around your place, and add some gun towers equipped with gatlin guns.

7. Our professors who are turning out today's corporate executives had best get away from the <u>cost</u> cutting formals to the <u>sales</u> formula (the old school approach).

8. I remember a quote that went sometimes like "Before you take away or destroy something –you better replace it with something of value." "Hold on Charlie Brown" yelled Cowboy, "that last thing you said don't make any sense to me". The Professor shot back – "Just look at all the little electronic gadgets (Iphones, tablets, etc.) that people are

making such a fuss over. I believe they are doing far more harm than good. They are destroying our communication industry along with hundreds of thousands of jobs in other areas. The next generation will be so dad gummed dependent on that stuff that there will be no one qualified to do any thinking." We are devolving.

9. To conclude, let me tell you the advice that I give all young folks:

*Enjoy whatever you do to earn a living - if you are unhappy - change:

*Give whatever you are doing your best.

*Save for the rainy day - whenever you get paid - pay yourself first - put a portion in a savings

account and don't touch it except for "emergencies".

*Don't try to do <u>everything</u> - i.e. - if you have a problem with plumbing - hire a plumber, etc.

*Go to church - and live a Christian life.

*Stay healthy and control your weight

*Exercise - the best I've found to be is "push backs" (when your appetite is satisfied - push

*Drink lots of water

CHAPTER 36

THE END OF THE TRAIL

The group had skipped their November meeting for several reasons. (1) Abe was sick (2) Thanksgiving (3) Cowboy had guests, and (4) the weather was bad. Abe died the night before the December meeting. Pinch was the first to arrive and he opened up the place, built a fire, and put on a pot of coffee. There was a knock on the door and when he opened the door a well dressed middle aged lady stepped in and induced herself. (She was Abe's daughter). She told Pinch of her father's death and said his body was at the funeral home in Bowie. Pinch expressed his condolences and said he would let the fire burn down and lock up the place. She insisted he not do that. She said one of her father's last concerns and wishes were that the club remain active and they continue to use the clubhouse which we had deeded to the club before his death. She had promised him she would try to see that happen - then she left.

Shortly thereafter the "members" began to arrive. One by one, Pinch told them of the death of Abe. Everyone was sad and suggested they cancel the meeting but Pinch told them what Abe's daughter had said so they decided to have the meeting – but only talk – no dominos today.

After everyone got their coffee and sat down Pinch said "The first thing we ought to do is elect a new President. Cowboy raised his hand and said "I nominate Pinch." Tony said "I second" Pinch said "I nominate Professor". Professor said "I don't want the job – let's vote." They voted with the following results:

Pinch – 5
Professor – 2

Pinch said, "I guess I'm it. Abe is at the funeral home in Bowie and I'll order flowers on behalf of the club. His funeral will be Tuesday at 10a.m. at the first Baptist Church in Bowie and I assume everyone will attend." They all nodded "Yes".

Pinch asked "What should we talk about today?" Stud spoke up and said "In the past I've talked to Abe about death and what a person needed to do to get ready for it – after all, it is inevitable." Abe claimed he had everything planned down to writing his own obituary." Pinch responded "According to his daughter that is true – she said that she was the administration of his will and in the large envelope containing his will was a small envelope addressed to her in which he had listed step by step what she needed to do. And by the way, he had deeded this building and an acre of land to this club."

"Let's just go around the room and let everyone describe what he has done to get ready for death. I'll start. "Said Pinch.

For starters, I do have a will. As all of you know I'm not married and have a sweet young thing living with me. I once was married to a wealthy widow but we got divorced. After the smoke cleared from that battle (divorce) I still had a few million dollars of stuff. My lawyer set up a trust for me that provides scholarships for poor kids in Fort Worth. I'm leaving most of my wealth to the synagogue in Decatur and of course I'm leaving a million to sweet thing. My lawyer (in Fort Worth) will administer my estate.

"What will happen to your ranch?" wistfully inquired Geek. Pinch almost said "I'll leave it to you and Bulldog" but didn't. He said "My lawyer will sell it and pay the tax then put the balance in the trust. I'm sure he will hire an auctioneer and sell all of my personal stuff and junk – after sweet thing takes whatever she wants." He looked at Billy and said "Cowboy, it's your turn."

Cowboy said "I ain't done nothing like Pinch described. Matter of fact, I didn't even understand what in the heck he was talking about." And since I ain't rich like him, I don't reckon it makes any difference no how."

Professor interrupted and said "It certainly does make a difference. If you would make an inventory of everything you own you will find you are worth a lot more than you think. For example, I would guess your ranch contains at least 4 sections of land, and land around her has gotten to be at least $2,000 per acres. A section is 640 acres so you have 2,560 acres @ $2,000 equals $5,120,000. "That ain't mine "Said Cowboy, "That is my wife's." The Professor said, then your wife absolutely needs some estate planning. The Professor said, "In Texas – half is yours. We are a community property state." If you do nothing, you are right – everything will go to your wife. "But I promised my truck, guns, and books to Bulldog "said Cowboy. "Verbal promises mean nothing" said the Professor – "I suggest you get a good lawyer and do some estate planning and write a will." "Anybody know a good lawyer?" asked Cowboy. "There are three or four good one in Bowie" answered the Professor. "Visit each of them and pick the one you like."

"That's a darn good idea" said Cowboy. I'm going to do that next week.

Pinch looked around the room and said "Tony, you are next in line – let's hear your story.

Tony said "As you all know, I am widowed and only have a daughter and granddaughter who will survive me. Plus my son-in-law of course. None of them are in need. My son-in-law is a doctor also and has a large salary. They live in a large expensive home in Dallas and my granddaughter will graduate from private school next year. I have already set up a scholarship trust for her and she wants to go to the University of Texas. In my will I am leaving the ranch and a couple of million in cash to my granddaughter and everything else to my daughter, who I named as executer of my will. Fairly simple stuff.

"Maybe so" said Pinch." But you know there will be a large estate tax to be paid." "Sure" said Tony. The lawyer who prepared my will computed the approximate amount and my liquid investments (stocks, cd's, bonds, etc.) will easily cover the estate tax.

"Sounds like you have everything covered" said Pinch. "Who's next."

Ace spoke up "Since you seem to be going clockwise around the circle I'm next in line – so here goes.

My situation is bit more complicated. I've been married three times and now live with the widow Smith who has tried very hard to get me to marry her – but I don't intend to. Two of my former marriages ended in bitter divorces and the other wife died. I have thirteen children and twenty grandchildren scattered all over this earth. All but one of my children are married. When I was living in Houston and working for NASA I met and developed a friendship with a lawyer who was a partner with a large law firm in Houston. He prepared an estate plan for me along with my will. Of course, I named him executer of my will and he understands the situation.

My children and their spouses and my grandchildren are in various economic situations. My first thought was to try to "balance" them out as best I could but the lawyer convinced me that was the wrong approach. This is basically how he has the will, etc set up.

My personal assets – there is a list "inventory" of my personal assets which includes cloths, coin collection, original art work, phones, gun collection, fishing gear, etc.

My children will, in turn, select what they want, beginning with the oldest child and going in the order of their age. The last one (younger) will pick two items and then the others will pick, one by one in age order (youngest oldest) until all have picked. Then the process will be repeated until all the items are gone.

Education funds – over the year I have made gifts to the grandchildren by paying for their college educations. The lawyer has a record of this and his next step will be to "even" up the education gifts to grandchildren – weather they went to college or not. For example, one grandson – Neil – went to medical school and I spent $200,000 on his education (the most of any) the lawyer will distribute money to each to bring them up to the $200,000. For example, another grandson George – joined the marines and did not go to college – he will get $200,000 cash.

Finally, the lawyer will convert everything else to cash, pay the bills and estate tax, then distribute the balance equally to my children. Let's assume the cash totaled $6,500,000 – each child would receive $500,000. ($6,500,000 ÷ 13) my ex wives are to receive <u>nothing</u>!

"You sound rather emphatic on that last point:" said Pinch.

"That's what a divorce will do for you" responded Ace.

The Geek and Bulldog where next in the circle but each said they had done nothing. So Pinch said "Professor – you get the final say."

The Professor said "What I have done is wrong. I'm glad we discussed this subject today – I have picked up some real good ideas and this week I plan to basically scrap what I have done and start all over."

"Why don't you explain your mistakes" suggested Pinch.

"Why not?" Answered the Professor. My situation is somewhat like Ace's except I don't have anywhere near the money he has. I have been married five times and have eight children and eight grandchildren. One of my marriages ended in an early annulment and one in a chaotic divorce. The other two divorces were hately contested and I've been married to my present (fifth) wife for a little over six years.

I must confess that I wrote my own will and left everything to my present wife and my children and named my wife as executor. I can see where there could be some battle over my meager estate – especially from one ex wife that comes to mind.

In the morning I'm going to Bowie and find a lawyer I like and drew up a will sort of along the line of Ace's will.

Pinch said "This was a good session and I think all of us learned something."

"I sure did learn something" spoke up Bulldog. "What is that? Asked Cowboy.

Bulldog answered "All of us will die someday – it's just a matter of time."

The end.

BOOKS WRITTEN BY
BILL R. THOMAS

Title	Brief Description
1) A Summer on Piney Creek	A Summer Spent with Friend Living in a Cave on Piney Creek (Kentucky)
2) Hickory Fired Tobacco, Moonshine Whiskey, Beautiful Horses, and Fast Women	Kentucky Based Short Stories
3) Bill T's Texas Bob Tales	Texas Based Short Stories
4) I Smell Smoke	Authors Experience as B-47 Crew Member in Strategic Air Command
5) My Most Memorable Adventures - One Hunting and One Fishing	Hunting Trip in Mexico and Fishing Trip in Alaska
6) The Accumulated Wisdom of the Bugscuffle Domino, Whittle and Spit Club	Philosophy and Wisdom Gained Over a Colorful Lifetime
7) The T-Bone Ranch	Developing a Cattle Ranch in Montague County, Texas
8) A Wild Shot In The Dark	Autobiography - Birth Through Air Force
9) The Debits Are On The Left, The Credits Are By The Window	Autobiography - Air Force to Present

Books may be purchased at - Lulu.com (Bill's Books)

www.ingramcontent.com/pod-product-compliance
Lightning Source LLC
Chambersburg PA
CBHW051550250626
47157CB00001B/255